This paperback edition publ

Copyright © J.M.G.Smith

Paperback ISBN 979-8-8649-524-74

This book is a work of fiction. Names, characters, places and incidents are either a product of the author's imagination or are used fictitiously. Any resemblance to actual people, living or dead, events or locales, is entirely coincidental.

Printed by Amazon

Santa Dash

J.M.G.Smith

Prologue

"All rise."

On cue, the room full of people stood up and waited in a respectful silence for the judge to gracefully exit. The moment she left; a quiet murmur of voices spread throughout as the people whispered amongst themselves. A short chubby woman in her early fifties and with horrific red dyed hair, pushed past the others congregated at the main door. The trial had all been too much for her, and the relentless constant waiting around was unbearable. She made her way to the waiting room and let the tears that she had been compressing, rush out in an uncontrollable torrent. A man silently entered and sat down near to her. Hurriedly she swept away the tears and pulled out her small compact mirror from her handbag. Realising how disarrayed her face was, she pulled out her full make-up set and began to apply powders and blushers to her cheeks.

"Sorry to interrupt you." He began, slightly smiling, "I didn't realise anyone was in here."

The woman gave a loud snort, "As if you couldn't hear me blubbering!"

There came a silence, the woman sighed, "Sorry. That was rude of me. I'm not myself."

"No need to apologise. Are you part of the Worthy trial?"

She gave a small nod, wiping mascara away from the corner of her eye and asked, "Are you?"

The man shook his head, "No. My friend was caught speeding for the umpteenth time. I'm waiting to pick him up. After this, he won't be allowed to drive for a long time yet. Has the trial finished yet?"

"Not yet. Waiting for the jury to come to a decision."

"Ah. That could be a while yet. Do you want coffee?"

She wobbled her head, "I won't leave this room or this building until I know the outcome."

"There's a coffee machine in the corner. I was going to buy you a coffee, could do with one myself," he chuckled.

"Oh…right." She responded, hating herself for being so stupid.

"Do you know Dylan Worthy then?"

"Not really. He used to be my daughter's boyfriend. They went out a couple of times. Until she dumped him and started dated Harry." She answered, then suddenly sat bolt upright, "Why are you asking me all these questions?"

"Sorry, didn't mean to interrogate. I'm just nosy, it's part of my job. D.S. Charlie Matthews."

"Margaret Taylor."

"Oh…I'm so sorry. I didn't know. I'm sorry for your loss."

"Weren't you on the case?" She mumbled, swallowing back tears.

"No…I was on another case. D.I. Jones was in charge of the Worthy case. I know all about it though. In my book he's definitely guilty. Accidental fire on a boat that has no gas? What a load of crap!" He concluded grumpily.

A voice came booming through the loudspeaker.

Margaret stood up with another loud sigh, "That'll be me. Wish me luck."

"Good luck," Charlie seriously responded.

The huddle of people from earlier reappeared from their various corners and made their way through the small door into the courtroom once more. Silently everyone found their seats from before and solemnly waited for the judge, the atmosphere sombre and depressing as a funeral.

"All rise."

The judge made her way to her podium and sat proudly upright on her seat, gave a short speech and called for the defendant. Dylan Worthy walked the few steps to the stand and stared unblinking into the distance, grinding his teeth in an effort to control his emotions.

"Dylan Worthy," The judge began, "You have been accused of indictment one, the manslaughter of Lisa Taylor. Members of the jury. How do you see fit to charge him? Guilty or not guilty?"

A woman of the jury boldly stood up and uttered, "We the jury, unanimously give the verdict, that Dylan Worthy is…not guilty of the manslaughter of Lisa Taylor."

"Dylan Worthy. You have been accused of indictment two, the manslaughter of Harry Lucas. Members of the jury. How do you see fit to charge him? Guilty or not guilty?"

"We the jury, unanimously give the verdict, that Dylan Worthy is…not guilty of the manslaughter of Harry Lucas."

A loud hubbub of protests rang out, as the families of the deceased broke down in angry tears, crying out for Dylan Worthy to be sent down. Calls were made for the trial to be redone and the jury accused, they were told they had got it all wrong and that they had been brainwashed by lies. It was a dark day for everyone, as Dylan was told he was free to go just before he headed back down the stairs.

"It's not right," Margaret Taylor mumbled to herself, "It's not right at all. If no-one is going to put a stop to this…then I will."

Part One

Chapter 1

The small village of Whitehaven glistened and shimmered in the golden light of a winter sun; sparkling frost evaporated into a thin mist under the sun's continuous hard glare. Badgers Farm was positioned just on the outskirts, a lonely desolate farmhouse sat neatly right in the middle of the farm. A herd of sheep huddled together for warmth in a field, were now being ordered to move by the repetitive barking of the sheepdogs that encircled them. The animals bumped and bustled each other in a bid to get away from the dogs that crept closer before suddenly moving away again. Two of the sheep broke free from the flock at last and headed away from the drama and towards the swollen river. An urgent ear-piercing whistle halted them in their tracks, as a tall thin man in country tweed and boasting greying hair, headed their way shouting,

"Go on! On with you!"

He waved his stick about, in an attempt to get the animals to turn around and head back to the farm. The sheep obliged, joining the others once more as they ambled into the barn, packed with warm and tempting straw and edible hay.

"That's the last one Jake."

Jake nodded, "Right. They're all accounted for."

The farmer wiped his forehead, "Right. Tea break. Then we'll look to the fields after."

The two men patted each other's shoulder in a friendly brotherly manner and strolled to the farmhouse. The farmer wasted no time in filling up the kettle and sticking it on the hob to boil and carefully popped two teabags into the teapot.

"Storm's brewing," he muttered, peering out of the window. "Those clouds couldn't get darker if they tried!"

"Mmm. We got the ewes and lambs home in time." Jake the farmhand agreed. He was slightly younger in age to the farmer, with no sign of grey yet in his dark hair. With well weathered skin and soft brown eyes, and a firmer athletic body from years of heavy lifting and hard work. He was certainly a looker and attracted many women, until he shooed them away by flashing his wedding ring.

"Maybe we should leave the fields for now." Ollie continued, "Plough them another time. You should go home Jake, be with your wife."

"I don't mind ploughing in a storm."

"There'll be flooding…you can guarantee it. The tractor will get stuck in the mud and then you'll be walking."

Jake sighed, "True."

The duo settled down to a quick cup of tea that was nowhere near hot enough and the digestive biscuits were too soft.

Jake eventually stood up, deciding that it was time to leave, "Alright. See you tomorrow, Ollie."

"Weather permitting," the farmer responded grimly. "Right, time to sort the girls."

Jake bobbed his head and shrugged into his jacket, walked out to his trusty motorbike and sped off back down the lane. Ollie ventured into the main barn just as the first pelt of rain came down, the cows in the barn sensed his arrival and mooed energetically.

The farmer laughed and rubbed one of them on the nose, "Good to see you too. Right, let's get to it."

Gently he led the cows to the dairy shed, lined them up and carefully yet firmly attached the pumps to their udders. Luscious creamy milk soon swiftly filled up the tanks. The storm outside grew heavier and the rain trickle soon became a small stream, as it seeped into the shed. The cows disliking the noise, stamped their hooves and bellowed aggressively. Ollie removed the pumps and guided them back to their warm barn, holding an arm in front of his face as the power of the wind pushed him back two steps. With a struggle he pushed the last cow in, then forced the barn door shut and swore to himself as the gale whipped the rope out of his hand. Quickly he darted forward and grabbed the rope and just as quickly tied the barn door handles together. By now, the farm had indeed flooded, as he predicted. The water gushed about his boots and the water level had almost risen to his ankles. At a half run, he made his way back up the short slope to his house and slammed the door shut.

"Phew," he muttered to himself and grabbed a pie from the fridge and placed it on a baking tray. The weather had peaked in intensity, as the rain lashed on the window. Just as he was about to place the savoury into the oven, something outside caught his eye, causing him to slam the pie back down, "Blummin' heck."

Lunging across the room he grabbed his phone and pressed a saved number, "Jake? Is that you? Come quick…it's an emergency! Jake…Jake?"

The electrics crackled, and with a pop the lights went out. The storm not only had cut off his phone line but the electrics also.

"Damn," Ollie swore, shrugging back into his jacket and waterproof trousers and shut the dogs into the kitchen. Bravely, he flung the front door open and headed back into the ferocious gale. Fortunately, the few sheep didn't get very far, as he rounded them up with his trusty stick, herding them back to the barn. The rest of the sheep were too terrified to leave their comfy home and watched uninterested at the ongoing drama outside. Ollie slammed the door shut and tied the rope on, thoroughly, double knotting for extra measure. By now it was pitch dark outside, and without the lights on in his farmhouse, he struggled to see where he was going. Dark shadows bounced around him and something large came towards him, not only large but loud too, letting off an eerie groaning noise. He had no time to react as the tree toppled down on top of him, crushing him down with a thump, flat out on his back. The farmer let out a moan as the dead feeling in his legs circulated his body. Ollie shut his eyes as he slipped into unconsciousness.

The following morning the storm had petered out into a gentle drizzle, the cows mooed with relief and the dogs in the kitchen barked and howled, scratching the door in earnest. It was the next door neighbour who found Ollie, with half his body crushed under the sycamore, stone cold. Hurriedly he pressed a finger to the farmer's neck and detected a faint heartbeat, he wasn't dead. Without a second thought he grabbed bundles of blankets from the house and covered Ollie, then rung for an ambulance and fire services. The ambulance couldn't reach him through the flooded road, so paramedics in waders made their way over with a stretcher and their gear strapped onto their backs. The fire brigade followed shortly after, and it didn't take long till they had assessed the situation.

"Ok, fortunately the tree has missed most of the farmer. We should be able to lift it off him without too much of a problem," one of the firemen proclaimed.

The paramedic in charge bobbed his head in agreement, "Ok. We'll keep him steady whilst you lift."

The firemen lined up and together as a team, managed to lift the heavy sycamore and held it in place whilst the ambulance team quickly pulled Ollie out. The tree was promptly released and crashed back down again, its flailing branches scratching a few men in the process.

"He's lucky to be alive," one of the paramedics murmured to his partner, as they carefully placed Ollie onto the flat piece of fabric. After fifteen minutes of fumbling around and making Ollie as comfortable as possible, they carefully made their way back down the road, and just as carefully they placed him into the back of the ambulance and slammed the doors shut. Without a second delay the vehicle sped off, rattling along the remainder of the bumpy track.

*

"Morning Mr Hart. How are we?"

"Alive." Ollie stated morbidly, turning his face away from the cheery nurse to look out the window.

"It's only a broken leg and pneumonia Mr Hart," the nurse chuckled, fluffing up the pillow. "It's a miracle you didn't break some ribs or any other part of your body, the way the tree fell on you like it did!"

Ollie grunted miserably, "Can I go home now? My animals need tending to."

"Not for a long time yet I'm afraid. Your farmhand Jake is looking after the animals, he came earlier but you were asleep," the nurse replied. "The animals are being well looked after. Now, how are you feeling? Is the morphine at the right level or do you need it stronger."

"I'm fine," Ollie again grunted, "Why didn't you wake me?"

"Sleep is important after surgery. Right…that's me done here. If you need someone or something, just ring the bell by your bed."

The farmer ignored her and rolled onto his side with his back to the nurse, he passionately hated hospitals, chock-a-block full of sick and dying people. The bedroom door promptly closed, and Ollie promptly fell asleep again. He was rudely awoken later that afternoon by the nurse once more making an appearance accompanied by his farmhand Jake.

"Why did you wake me?" He grumbled irritably.

"Well, I like that! Earlier you got upset with me because I *didn't* wake you…now you're upset because I *did* wake you!" The nurse retaliated moodily and huffily stormed out of the room.

Jake chuckled as he closed the door, "I can see you've upset your nurse already! I brought some grapes."

"Typical cliché. What's happening on the farm? Is it badly flooded? And the animals?" Ollie asked anxiously, painfully pulling himself upright.

"Calm yourself, everything is ok. The fields are seriously flooded as you predicted but the animals are fine, they're safe."

"No thanks to you." The farmer mumbled, pulling his sheets higher up over his cold arms.

"What's that supposed to mean?" Jake asked with confusion.

"Just that. It's your fault I'm here."

"Meaning what, exactly?"

"You didn't tie the barn handles together with rope…did you? Some of the sheep got out."

Jake paled as he realised his mistake, "I didn't think."

"No…you didn't. And you didn't cut the tree down either…it was a major hazard on the farm. And I asked you countless times!"

"Hey! That's hardly my fault! It's your farm and your tree! You should have cut it down yourself!" Jake angrily retaliated. "Anything else? How about a thank you, for looking after the animals whilst you're stuck in hospital!"

"You're fired Jake." Ollie calmly announced, glaring at his farmhand.

"Wait…what?" Jake stammered, "You can't fire me. I'm your best friend and the best farmhand you've ever had. You wouldn't manage without me."

"I'll find someone else. Someone who won't keep making stupid mistakes! Like that time the cows got out and blocked the main road into the village. Or the time you left the combine harvester out in the rain, and it rusted over. Or the time you forgot to take the sheep to market and lost me a lot of money!"

"Ok…so I made a few simple mistakes."

"*Costly* mistakes Jake! I'm sorry. But I've made my decision. The farm isn't making enough money as it is, and mistakes like this keep setting me back."

"Right," Jake agreed amiably, even though his heart was racing with defeat, "Well…that's that then. I'll look after the animals till you return, and I'll be on my way."

Ollie suddenly felt overwhelmed with guilt as he looked at Jake's deflated face, "Hang on…how about you stay until I find someone else. If you prove your worth, I'll let you stay on."

Jake mood suddenly uplifted, "Thank you Ollie. I won't let you down again. Anyhow, I'd better let you rest. The nurse said ten minutes and it's been more than that. And the cows will need milking again soon."

"Bye Jake."

"Yeah…bye for now."

Chapter 2

Badgers Farm was still inaccessible as Jake parked his motorbike in the lane and crossed the flooded fields in his thick gumboots. It didn't take long till the cows were fully milked, and with the animals all fed and checked over, he made his way back home. The farm had six small cottages, perched right on the edge of the land, each house named after a flower. Primrose Cottage was light sandy pink in colour, with a cottage garden full of blooms surrounding it; but being winter, most of those blooms had died down for the year. Jake unlatched the gate underneath the archway full of cut back roses and ambled down the cobbled path to his bright pink door. The smell of roast chicken and seasoned vegetables greeted him, as he pulled his boots and mac off.

"Mmm," he said, sniffing the air, "Something smells good!"

"Nothing like a roast on a Sunday," his wife replied, popping a spoon into his mouth, "What do you think of the gravy? I made it myself. Is it too runny? Too thick? Salty?"

"Nope, it's perfect." Jake responded. His stomach rumbled with hunger. "How's the baby?"

"Shouldn't be too long now. Had a few false contractions today." Maisy answered, pushing her hands into the oven mitts and pulled the chicken out. "Yep, all done!"

"You're positively glowing!" Jake laughed, retrieving the carving knife from the drawer. "What was your day like?"

The duo sat down at the laid table and proceeded with their extremely late lunch. Jake had lit a small fire, which was now emitting warmth and cosiness and added to the romance, as the weather once more turned cold and brutal.

"What's wrong Jake?" Maisy gently asked, tidying away the empty plates. "You've hardly said a word all through lunch."

"Nothing's wrong. Why would anything be wrong? I'm just enjoying this amazing meal, that's all." Jake wiped his mouth with a napkin and grinned, "Time to wash up, and you can put your feet up for once."

Maisy sighed defeated, she knew there was no getting through to him or making him reveal what was going on in his mind. Making herself a lemon tea, she withdrew to the living room and put on the television. She must have fallen asleep for it was now dark outside, and something behind her caused her to stir from her slumber. Jake was wrestling his arms into his damp coat that clung tightly to his shirt.

"Where are you going?" his wife asked, rubbing her dazed eyes.

"Mum's." Jake simply replied, "If you need me, call her number. I don't hear my phone when I'm round hers."

"But Jake…it's late." Maisy whimpered, looking at the clock on the mantlepiece. "Is she expecting you?"

"She is now. I'll see you later."

*

Rita Byrd was extremely surprised to find her son on her doorstep and was very reluctant to let him in so late. Jake reassured her he wouldn't be staying long and flopped onto the sofa, exhausted from such an emotional turmoil of a day. The home comforts of his youth enveloped him and reminded him how much he missed the home he grew up in. Why did he ever leave?

"Hellooooo?"

Ahh, thought Jake, that's why. Ben Byrd. A notorious pain in the neck, a troublemaker, a ladies man, mummy's golden boy, mummy's gentle giant. His stocky build now filled the door frame, and his giant hands gracefully pushed a brown lock of hair away from his dazzling sea blue eyes.

"Hey up bro! Thought I heard you voice," Ben guffawed, smacking Jake playfully on the back, "What brings you to mummy's house?"

"Why aren't you in the pub?" Jake retaliated, glaring at his younger brother.

"Why aren't you?"

"Because I don't want to."

"Cool," Ben agreed, "I don't want to, either."

Jake's mother popped her head around the door, "Will you be staying for dinner Jake? It's cottage pie."

"No thanks mum, can't stay long. Maisy will worry." Jake responded, only just realising how late it was as the clock chimed 8pm.

"How rude!" Ben stated, frowning at his older brother, "Turn up uninvited and then refuse mummy's dinner!"

"FINE! Fine. I'll stay. Thank you, mum."

The three of them settled down at the table, Jake felt relieved he gave into his brother, the cottage pie smelt and looked amazing, as he poured more gravy on the top.

"What brings you over so late Jake?" Rita asked her son, "You haven't said."

"It doesn't matter." Jake mumbled, trying to push the soft carrots onto his fork.

"So, you came all this way, late at night, to tell me nothing's wrong?"

"Look, I'll tell you later mum."

"No. You'll tell me now!"

"Yes!" Ben piped up, enjoying his mother belittling his older brother. "Tell mummy what's wrong Jake. She's worrying about you now, and it's your fault! So, tell her what's wrong and put our poor mummy out of her misery."

"Just butt out of it Ben! It's got nothing to do with you!" Jake snapped, slamming his cutlery down on the plate. And seeing his mother's sad worried face, he finally caved in, "Fine. I got fired at work today. Sort of…that is. He wants me to prove myself worthy, otherwise he'll find someone else."

"You're hanging onto your job by a thread? Is that what you're saying?" His elderly mother enquired, feeling fatigued. "I was relying on you to look after me Jake. I'm too old now to get another job, and I've spent all my life savings on this place. What will I do now?"

"Me and Maisy can still help financially. Don't worry mum. And what about Ben? Why can't Ben help you?"

"Ben?" Rita asked confused, "But Ben is helping. He cooks, he cleans. He does the weekly shopping, he washes the laundry. Does the bins, feeds the cats. Do I need to go on?"

"No mum," Jake sighed. "I meant, can Ben help financially?"

"How? Without a job?"

"Why can't Ben get a job then? He's forty next month!"

"He's working hard enough as it is without pinning down a job."

Ben interrupted with a dramatic sigh, "Ok big bro. I'll get a job. If it helps our mummy, I'll do it."

"But Ben…I need you here. How will I manage without you?" Rita stuttered, wringing her hands.

"I'll get you a carer mum." Jake reassured her, gently rubbing her back. "Ben will get a job and help financially that way. Sound good?"

"So…you want your brother to get a job, to help pay for a carer to look after me. When he is already working as a carer for me, for free? I don't understand Jake, you want Ben to *pay* someone else to do his job? Why aren't you paying Ben then to do his job? Why are you letting Ben work for me for free? You should be paying him."

Jake exploded with frustration, "RIGHT! If you need me! I'll be…AT THE PUB!"

He fiercely pulled his coat of the coat rack, rammed his feet home into his shoes and stormed out of the door.

His mother quietly closed the door, "Was it something I said?"

*

The Fox and Rabbit of Whitehaven sat conveniently in the middle of the village, an old cottage type of pub with thatch roofing and shallow windows. Windows which were misted up with condensation, as people sweltered from the heat emitting from the large open fire at the far end of the room. The previous owner of the pub had died eons ago and passed the ropes onto his last remaining son and his wife, a middle aged couple who had no clue what they were doing. However, it didn't take long till they had sussed it out and were now professionals and well liked in the village. Always heartily greeting people, whatever the weather and whatever mood they were in, everyone got a warm welcome. Jake moodily pushed the door open a little bit too roughly and banged the door into a wooden post. A couple sitting by the entrance jumped with surprise and the man accidentally knocked his drink onto the floor.

"Easy Jake!" The publican called out, heading over towards him with a mop in hand and proceeded to clean up the mess. "What's got into you?"

Jake ignored him and headed up to the bar and perched himself on a stool and brooded over the counter. The pub owner profusely apologised to the gentleman on Jake's behalf, promising him and his wife a free drink on the house.

"Cheer up Jake. It's not the end of the world," the publican's wife joked. "Is it that brother of yours again?"

Jake glumly nodded, "As always. Mum didn't help either. She properly worships that dope!"

"Pour that sad man a pint Jackie!" The publican joked, jumping up onto the stool next to Jake. "Don't let Ben get you so down all the time."

"Easy for you to say Nick. He's not your brother."

Nick's wife Jackie rang the little bell by the counter, "Last orders please."

Nobody moved. Jackie poured out a pint for Jake and proceeded to tidy up the bar and clean up the pumps.

"Ollie is thinking of letting me go. He's given me a second chance. Just got to make sure now that I don't cock it up again! I'm telling you this because it's only a matter of time before Ben comes here to gloat!" Jake explained, taking a swig.

Nick tugged his moustache puzzled, "You're Oliver's best farmhand! What is he thinking of letting you go for? He won't manage the farm without you!"

"Thanks. He's looking for another farmhand in the meantime, someone who won't let him down."

Nick snorted, "Good luck to him, finding someone better than you!"

Jackie rang the bell once more, "Time people."

Jake nodded and finished off his beer, "Thanks."

"You'd best get home to that wife of yours," said Jackie, staring at him fondly, taking his empty glass away.

An elderly man at the far end of the bar, unsteadily clambered off his stool, and wobbled for a second on his feet. With a hiccup, he yanked his jacket off the stool and swung it full force over the counter, sending pieces of paper flying everywhere. The man turned and faced Nick, "Sorry about that. Be seeing you Nick."

Nick sighed and murmured quietly under his breath, "Not again!"

Jackie stopped him from walking over and said, "I'll tidy it away. You can put the chairs up."

Jake offered her a hand, "What's all this for?"

"Our Santa fun run. You know…we've done one every year for the past eleven years."

Jake picked one up to read, "Saturday 10th December. Wear your best Santa costume, a prize will be given for the best looking Santa. A three mile loop through the village, run or walk. All money raised will go to St Heliers Hospital."

Jackie looked sad for a moment, "It's been thirteen years now. George should have celebrated his 21st birthday last month."

Nick must have overheard for he swiftly came over and joined her side, "It wasn't your fault. We told him multiple times not to go out on the lake, but he wouldn't listen."

Jake quietly asked, "Is that where…?"

Jackie nodded, "Yes. It's where he fell in. The ice was too thin, and he just went through. Poor Harvey…he did everything he could to save his best friend. Risked his own life to save him, but it was too late."

"I'm sorry. I remember your son George. Always was a wanderer going off on adventures with Harvey. Do you remember they made a wild camp on the farm? When Ollie found them, they had made a makeshift campfire and were eating cold beans from a can!"

Jackie laughed, "Sounds about right. So…will you be there? We're starting and ending at the pub."

Jake bobbed his head, "You can count on me. I'll put some more flyers up for you around the village and a few in the big towns. Hopefully we'll get more people than last year."

Nick agreed, "Sounds good. If we can get more than five people this year, I'll be extremely happy with that."

"Right, best be off. Thanks mate. I'll see you."

"Bye Jake," Nick replied, watching him leave before shutting the door and locking it up tight.
"Phew…what a night! Best go find the old Santa suit then."

"And I'll find my Mrs Claus outfit," Jackie replied with a laugh.

Chapter 3

Jake woke up to another cold day, the windows of his little cottage had delicate ice patterns formed on the cold glass. He traced the flakes with his finger, admiring the symmetry, when his wife walked in.

"Is it today Ollie comes home?" she asked.

Jake nodded and sat down to breakfast, "I thought we could pick him up after your hospital appointment."

Maisy agreed with him, "That's a good idea."

A little robin flew down and pecked away at the bird feed scattered on the ground, soon a flurry of birds joined him, until they were swiftly chased away by a naughty squirrel.

"Beautiful morning," Maisy hummed, "Right, best get going."

It was a long drive to Gresham hospital, but they made it just in time, and the check-up was over in a couple of minutes, and they were soon on their way. They headed over to the ward where Ollie was recovering, he wasn't there.

"Oliver Hart?" Jake asked one of the nurses, "Are we in the right place? We were supposed to meet him here."

"I'll just go and ask someone," she responded, and deftly left the room at a speedy pace.

It took a good ten minutes until another nurse entered the room, a senior nurse from the looks of it. She eyed Jake and his wife with suspicious blue eyes,

"Mr Hart was discharged last night. A young man picked him up, I think it was his son."

"Ollie doesn't have children," Jake replied bewildered, "He asked me to come and get him today."

"I'm sorry. But he's not here. He's gone home and so should you."

"Right…of course. Thank you."

Jake took his wife's hand and led her back to the car, just in the nick of time too, as the time on the ticket was almost up.

"What was all that about?" Maisy asked, clambering into the Jeep, "I thought you had arranged everything last night."

"We did…thought we did. Maybe we crossed wires somehow. Listen…don't worry about it. Let's get you home, shall we?"

*

Lunch time soon came and went, Jake decided it was best he headed back to the farm once more, see if Ollie got home in one piece. As he turned the corner and parked his bike in the little shack, he was shocked to see the tractor; which he had carefully locked up in the main barn last night, was now parked outside it. Could Ollie have moved it? With his broken leg still healing? Jake quickly dismissed that idea and ventured into the main barn itself to retrieve some hay for the sheep, only to find a couple of the bales missing. There was no way that the farmer could have climbed up the wooden rungs on the ladder, it was impossible. He must have had some help. But why would he ask someone else for help when he had a trusty farmhand just round the corner. Jake had a sinking feeling in the pit of his stomach, he remembered that Ollie was looking for someone else to help him, someone who supposedly could do a better job. How did he find someone that quickly though? The sheep in the barn next door looked up at Jake and baaed contently as he strode past, hellbent on seeking out the new help in earnest. There was a sudden loud ruckus of squawking and clucking from outside, Jake immediately knew what that was, somebody was feeding the chickens. He raced back to the yard as fast as he could, only to be met with another nasty surprise.

"YOU!?" He blurted angrily, marching over furiously with his fists clenched, "WHAT ARE YOU DOING HERE!?"

"Jake!" A voice called out from the dairy, "What are you doing? Shouting at my new farmhand."

"Your new…wait. What's going on?" Jake stammered, taking a sudden step back.

"That's right bro. I'm the new help. You said that Ollie needed a new helper, so here I am…helping." Ben smirked triumphantly, scattering more grain at his feet. "I've fed and milked the cows for you too. Poor things were mooing so uncomfortably, I had to relief them."

Jake's face reddened, as he realised with everything going on that morning, he had completely forgotten to milk them, hiding his embarrassment he retaliated rudely, "What do you know about cows? Or farming for that matter?"

"Plenty. I've learnt a lot from you for a start. You're always going on and on about what you're doing all day at work…I picked up a thing or two."

"It's hard work. Are you sure you're up to it? You've never worked a hard day in your life!"

"Now Jake," the farmer called out, hobbling over to join them, "Be reasonable. He'll manage, little steps at a time. Just be grateful we have another hand to help us. I don't know why you didn't mention your brother when I said I need another farmhand to help. He's been extremely useful to me this morning. Where were you this morning Jake?"

"Hospital appointment with Maisy. And then we looked for you…to take you home….as we agreed. Do you remember?"

"Ah," said Ollie, "Your brother picked me up last night, he was in the hospital at the time. Two birds one stone."

"Oh, so he just happened to be there, did he?"

"Come on Jake," Ben interrupted, "Let's be civil about all this. Now I've got to get back to work. The dairy needs a good clean. Do you want to take the tractor to the bottom field? The field needs prepping before we plant the potatoes."

"Don't tell me how to do my job," Jake snapped, "I was just about to do that myself!"

Ben goaded, "Don't forget to wash the tractor afterwards. It was in a horrifically muddy state earlier. Took me half the morning to wash it down."

Ollie sighed as he handed Jake the keys to the tractor, mumbling to himself, "This is going to be a long day."

*

With the last of the mud carefully washed off the plough, Jake wheeled the machinery inside and carefully locked the doors, checking twice before hanging the keys up in the farmhouse. It was suspiciously quiet, not even a peep stirred from the farm animals. The setting sun cast long eerie shadows over the land; a leaf rustled as it blew across the path. There was no sign of his annoying brother or the farmer. Jake sighed and decided to lock up the farm for the night, just as the last of the light disappeared for the day and darkness settled in. Maisy was pleased to see him, and then quickly disgruntled as he announced he had plans to meet a couple of friends at the pub.

"Fine! Go!" she moodily retaliated and headed upstairs for an early night. Jake wasn't in the mood for an argument, and the moment dinner was eaten, he ventured out into the night, leaving his bike behind. The Fox and Rabbit was once again, warm and inviting, hearty laughter could be heard from inside and he wondered what was going on. He pushed the door open, gentler this time and was met with an awful scene before his very eyes.

"YOU!?" he roared, snorting heavily with rage.

"Why do you always shout 'YOU!' every time you see me? Our mother gave me a name." Ben laughed, chugging back the rest of his beer. "Another one Ollie?"

"Don't mind if I do," Ollie laughed, passing over his almost finished glass, "Come join us, Jake."

"No…thanks. I won't. You sound pissed Ben. How long have you been propping up the bar?" Jake asked curiously.

Ben thought for a moment, "Since this afternoon. I finished my chores and Ollie can't do much in his state, so I offered him a beer."

"Then…what? You go to my local? Why can't you go to your usual pub The King's Head?"

"It might be *your* local, but it's not *your* pub! Anyone can come here, it's a free country. Isn't that right Nick?"

Nick not wanting to be involved in the silly bickering, subtly bobbed his head, "He does have a point, Jake."

"Whatever," Jake silently huffed and took himself into the snug at the end of the pub. The unruly laughter picked up again, Jake angrily folded his arms. Ollie had never agreed to go for a pint with him, so why say yes to his stupid brother?

"Hello? I heard you were in here."

"Dan! Good to see a true friend. We are still friends…yes?" Jake asked worriedly.

Daniel and Jake had been friends for five years now, having met in the same place they were now locally drinking in. Dan Cooper was a gardener by trade, but with the winter drawing in and less customers to serve, his trade was slowly dwindling, and less money was coming in.

Dan laughed as he sat down, then absentmindedly scratched mud off his steel capped boots, "Stupid question. What's got into you? And why is Ben being overfriendly with your boss?"

"Ben wants my job. He won't get it through skill and experience obviously, so he's doing what he's best at and kissing Ollie's…"

"Ok, ok. I get it," Daniel butted in, "No need for crudeness! Shall we go somewhere else? King's Head?"

"Might as well, it'll be better than here!" Jake agreed, grabbing his coat and rudely pushed past the congregation at the bar.

"Leaving so soon Jake?" Ben jeered, throwing a few crisps at his brother. "I'll see you soon."

"What's that supposed to mean?" Jake furiously turned to face him.

"Just that…" Ben gestured with his eyebrows by raising them up and down in quick succession, "You'll see."

Daniel pushed Jake towards the entrance, "Ignore him. He just wants to start a fight, probably wants to get you banned from the pub."

The duo headed out and towards the outskirts of the village, zipping their coats up to the very top, as the icy winds attempted to freeze them. The King's Head was unpleasant and much noisier than The Fox and Rabbit; the crash of snooker cues hitting the balls and roars of triumph as Manchester United won a goal. Jake sat down at an inconspicuous table by the window at the other side near the toilets. A loud growl by his feet however, made him leap up in alarm.

"Can't sit there," an old haggard trampy looking man grumbled, "Dog don't like it. Do you Dog?"

The dog looked up at his master and growled in Jake's direction and let out a loud bark.

Jake didn't waste another second and chose another table, far away from 'Dog' as possible.

Daniel joined him a minute later, "They charge a fortune here. It was a whole pound more for your drink."

"That's all right. Don't want to be here longer than necessary," Jake replied, scooping froth off his beer. A riot broke out between two men at the bar, the barman firmly stepped in and booted the pair out the back door. Jake tutted, "What a dumpy place."

"And Ben comes here regularly, does he? Why are those kinds of people attracted to places like this? Glad Izzy didn't want to come."

"Where is Izzy?"

"At home probably. We broke up."

"Again?"

Daniel suddenly looked downtrodden, "It's over between us, for real this time. She's moved on."

"Oh," Jake responded, unsure what to say, "Who's she with now?"

"Dunno. She's meeting him tomorrow in Gresham at that new pizza place off the square."

There was a silence between the two friends, another loud outburst broke out at the bar, followed by another scuffle.

Daniel finished off his beer, "We should follow them."

Jake looked at his friend bewildered, "What? Who?"

"Izzy. Find out who the new bloke is."

"Are you mad? If she sees you, you'll be in a heap of trouble. Why can't we just ask her?"

"Whatever," Daniel sighed and whipped out his phone and with ferocious speed texted his ex-girlfriend, Jake ordered another round whilst he waited for the outcome. After ten minutes Dan flung his phone down and let out an antagonised groan, "She won't tell me anything. She's complaining I'm too clingy and possessive and that she needs a break."

"Ok. That's that then. I'm going home."

"Will you join me tomorrow?"

"Where?"

"To the square in Gresham of course, where else?"

Jake sighed and shook his head, "Izzy's right about you. You're far too clingy. Move on already."

"Only when I find out who the new bloke is…then I'll move on."

"Right. Night Dan…oh no."

With lightning speed Jake ran towards the fire exit at the back of the pub and escaped, just as Ben ambled through the front, cool as a cucumber. Daniel not wanting to be greeted by Jake's brother also left via the back door. A short chubby woman with her red dyed hair plaited back, watched them leave with interest, as she scribbled some more notes into her book.

Chapter 4

The last cloud disappeared from sight and the moon reappeared, a small slither of a crescent and yet it still shone ghostly white. Daniel wound down his car seat further, not wanting to be seen dithering in his vehicle. It had been half an hour and Isabelle was still pacing around in her room. Her petite silhouette could easily be seen behind the thin curtain as she tried on various dresses. A car pulled up right in front of Dan's. Dan ducked down even further as the bright beams from the vehicle shone right over his head, fortunately the driver was distracted and whistled a merry tune as he hopped out of the car. There was a loud rap on a front door which was soon opened a second later and pleasantries exchanged, Dan immediately recognised Isabelle's voice and realised that the driver must be the new bloke. Cautiously he raised his head to take a peep, unfortunately for him it was too dark to see anything. Isabelle and the new guy wasted no time in getting going, the car had revved up and driven off before Dan had time to put his car seat back into a driving position. Daniel cursed and quickly started his car and drove off after them; it was too late, they were already gone. He debated for a moment whether Isabelle was telling the truth and that they really were going to Gresham for a date. It was a good half an hour drive; bit excessive just to go out for pizza when there was a pleasant pizzeria in the next town over.

"Dammit!" he said to himself, as he cruised his car towards the fork, then mumbled, "Left, or right?"

The car behind him hooted impatiently. Daniel sighed, "Left it is."

The journey took longer than he had hoped, nearly an hour altogether by the time he had found a decent parking spot in the city. Market Square sat conveniently in the middle of the hustle and bustle, Ziggy's Pizzeria was well lit up and 'newly opened' posters decorated the windows. It was hard to see inside with the posters stuck over the frosted glass, he couldn't see Isabelle or her new bloke anywhere. Daniel knew the only way to get a good look in was to head inside the pizzeria itself. Subtly he sneaked through the main doors and noticing an absence of staff to welcome him in, he edged along the wall towards the back of the restaurant, whilst summing up the diners.

"Can I help you sir? Have you booked a table?" a young Greek female waitress asked, eyeing him curiously.

Daniel chuckled sheepishly, "No. No, I haven't booked."

"Table for one, is it? We have one table left. This way."

Daniel pulled his hoodie up over his head, bewildering the waitress even further, as he was led to an inconspicuous table in the corner. Luck was on his side, his table was positioned right next to the VIP area, and he could just about make out his ex-girlfriend. She was laughing merrily as the guy opposite cracked another lame joke and pretended his napkin was an aeroplane. The guy must be loaded with money to afford such luxury, as another bottle of champagne was brought to their table. Typical Izzy, Daniel muttered to himself, always after a man with money; that must be the real reason for the break up, not his clinginess but the fact he had made little trade with his gardening business and not much money had come into his pocket in the last couple of months. Who was this new guy anyway? Apart from having a lot of money, he was clearly hitting middle age, same as him. The receding hair line and the greying temples, the small chin and the wide spaced out eyes, a round belly which wobbled every time he laughed. There was nothing attractive about him at all apart from his wealth!

The waitress had returned with her pen poised, "What can I get you sir?"

Daniel coughed and mumbled, "A pear cider with a Fiorentina pizza please."

Isabelle stopped laughing and turned to peer in his direction, Daniel quickly ducked under the table, pretending he had dropped his phone.

"Anything else?" The waitress snapped, clicking her pen vigorously.

"None, thank you."

She briskly left and made her way to the bar. Daniel followed her with his eyes and noticed to his delight that the toilets were situated right next to Izzy's table. Picking up a menu to conceal his face, he made his way past the couple and sauntered into the small hallway. Finally, he could hear some of their conversation; apart from the fact that they had stopped talking and were now holding hands and looking into each other's eyes.

"Come on," he grumbled quietly and impatiently to himself. A man walked out of the men's toilets and gave Daniel a queer stare as he headed back to his table. Eventually Isabelle's date opened his mouth to say something.

"I love you Isabelle," he mooned across the table, causing Isabelle to splutter on the salad sauce.

"Easy Joe. This is only our first date. How about we get to know each other better first." Isabelle smoothly replied.

"But we already know each other. All those chats we've already had."

"That was just casual talk when I was working. You know…polite conversation."

"Are you saying you don't love me?"

Daniel looked on and made a face of disgust, Isabelle only had one love in her life and that was him.

Isabelle awkwardly tugged on her long hair, "I don't love you…yet. But I do like you, Joe."

Joseph chuckled, "Good enough for me. Right. Dessert?"

"Not for me. I'm full, that was a lovely meal. If you excuse me, I need to head to the ladies."

Daniel quick as lightning dashed into the men's toilets, he paused for a moment, then headed back to his own table, he had heard enough. Joseph noticed him cruising past and yet was oblivious to his identity. There was a cold pizza on the table waiting for Daniel and a flat cider. Hastily he threw down a twenty pound note and withdrew from the restaurant and lingered outside for a moment, deciding what to do next. The waitress from earlier was hanging in the alley, smoking lazily on a cigarette when she spotted Dan.

"Hey! Hey you!" she called out.

Dan wasted no time in making a run for it, enough was enough for one night.

*

Dan woke up with a shock, as a fast repetitive knock sounded on his window. Cramps and a sharp pain in his back awoke his senses, feeling dazed he opened his car door.

"Have you been sleeping in your car all night? Outside *my* house!?" An angry female voice commanded.

Daniel groaned and rubbed his tired eyes, he hadn't intended to fall asleep, it must have happened whilst he was waiting for the couple to return.

"You know, you're turning into a right stalker you are," the voice continued, "I know it was you last night in the restaurant, I saw you leave."

"Izzy," Dan drawled, "I'm not a stalker, I just love you. I wanted to make sure you were safe meeting this new guy. What do you even know about him?"

"Not a lot. That's the whole point of going out on a date! To get to know someone better."

"You have me Izzy. You don't need to date anyone else, I know you love me Izzy."

"Grow up Dan! Stop being so clingy and thinking you own me!" Isabelle snapped, pulling her dressing-gown tighter around her thin body.

"Just fill me in and reassure me that he is the right person for you." Daniel pleaded.

Izzy sighed aggressively, "Fine! Joe's a headteacher in Slapton, he works at the High School."

"Slappy High? He works at that dump!"

"Let me finish! He's thirty-five, never been married and no kids. He lives just down the road from me…Anything else?"

"How long are you planning on seeing him?"

"You're unbelievable! Goodbye Dan! And I never want to see you again!" Isabelle retorted angrily and ran back into her house, deliberately slamming the door behind her.

Daniel sighed and closed his car door, placed the key in the ignition and pushed the gear stick into drive. He irritability mumbled under his breath, "I'll be back, she'll be sorry she ever met Joe."

*

Jake propped up his feet onto the little pouffe, slurped noisily from his bottle of beer and tuned himself into the television. It had been one very long and trying day, his brother Ben had been continuously in his face, doing all the farm chores and taking all the praise from Ollie. The hair on his skin still prickled with irritation. Why couldn't Ben just disappear from the earth? Jake's phone vibrated and chimed, alerting him to an incoming message, it was Dan. A second later, there came a pounding on his front door.

"Alright!" Jake shouted, wriggling out of his comfy position, "No need to break down the door!"

The banging continued right up until Jake flung the door open, "What's with the noise!?"

"Sorry. It's been a long day." Daniel apologised, removing his dusty steel capped boots.

"Beer?"

Dan accepted the beer gratefully and flopped onto the sofa, "Where's Maisy?"

"At her mum's."

"Oh ok." Dan replied dumbly, rubbing his forehead distraughtly, "Why did Isabelle leave me Jake? Did I come on too strong? Is it my deodorant? Or the fact I only shave once a week, or don't go the gym. Maybe I didn't buy her enough presents? Or take her out somewhere romantic? Apparently, this 'Joe' of hers is swooping her off to Italy next month, first to Venice then Rome then Milan. I saw Izzy this morning and again at Gresham Mall today, buying clothes and stuff for the trip."

"Come off it Dan, you're crowding her. Give that poor girl a break already. Give me a break already for that matter!" Jake commanded, then flicked over the channel, "Find someone new and move on."

"I can't. God! I hate this 'Joe'! Where did he come from anyhow and how did she find him?"

"Dating website, I imagine."

"Why can't he just go back to the hole he came from. I wish he never existed!"

"I wish Ben never existed," Jake grumbled, heading to the kitchen for another beer.

"What's your stupid little brother done now? Is he still at the farm?"

"Unfortunately." Jake answered subduedly, "He's been working his ass off and receiving high praise from Ollie. He even felled down another 'dangerous' tree near the farmhouse and said, *'Don't want any more accidents Ollie, don't want you back in hospital'*. I'll give him an accident!"

Daniel guffawed, "You don't really mean that, do you?"

Jake silently pondered for a second before ramming his hand down the back of the sofa, his hand grasped an object, which he slowly pulled out of its hiding place.

"Whoa Jake! What the hell are you doing with that!?" Dan exclaimed, jumping up in alarm and knocked his bottle over, "It's not loaded, is it?"

Jake laughed and turned the gun over in his hands, "Don't crap yourself. It's a replica. Pretty neat don't you think?"

"What are you planning to do with it?" Dan suspiciously questioned, sitting back down.

"Give Ben a scare. He's planning on taking part in the Santa fun run this Saturday, wants to beat me. Naturally, I'll show him the gun and give him a *proper* run for his money!" Jake chuckled, throwing the gun onto the coffee table.

Daniel laughed maliciously with him, then thoughtfully picked up the gun, "Actually, can I borrow this for a bit?"

"Suppose so. But don't go waving it about in public! The police will shoot you dead if you're not careful."

A whistling noise resounded outside, a deep eerie ear piercing sound that a grave digger might make when doing the night rounds. Men called to each other in the darkness as a truck or lorry pulled up right outside the house, doors slammed shut and the grating noise of a metal door being pushed up followed. Jake wasted no time and leapt up to peer out from the side of the curtain,

"I don't believe it!"

Furiously he banged his front door open and marched down the little path, pushed his sleeves up his arm and flexed his biceps. Daniel heard the commotion outside and quickly rammed the gun in his back pocket and tied his coat around his waist to conceal the weapon. The removal men hovered awkwardly unsure what to do next, as the two brothers lunged at each other and tackled on the ground. One of the men eventually plunged in and dragged Ben off Jake, releasing his strangling hold on Jake's throat. Jake coughed and spluttered, swinging his arm round to clock Ben in the face. The second removal man quickly grabbed his arm and pulled him up onto his feet,

"THAT'S ENOUGH!" He roared, pushing Jake away from the action.

Ben sniggered then sneered, wiping blood off his lip, "Not a nice way to greet your new neighbour."

"What are you talking about Ben?" Dan demanded stepping outside onto the threshold, so he could glare at him with pierced eyes.

"Oh, sorry. Didn't Ollie say? He's given me Ivy Cottage. I'm his new farmhand."

The ground shook beneath Jake's feet, giddy with shock he spluttered, "What!? What?"

"Mmm," Ben continued smugly, "Now, if you excuse me…I'll be moving into my new home. I really hope we can be friends. Not only will we be working together, but we'll also be living next door to each other. Wasn't it you who suggested I get a job? Oh, mummy will be so proud!"

Shaking from anger Jake marched straight back indoors; Dan not wanting to be left outside quickly followed suit. Ben smugly grinned behind their backs knowing he had won the battle, the removal men wasted no more time and soon were on their way, glad that the night was over. Meanwhile, Jake paced aggressively in his living room, then pounded with his fists on the sofa.

"Where's the gun Dan!?" Jake barked angrily. "Where is it!?"

"I have it, don't worry. Now, don't do anything stupid, ok? We'll show him one day. Then he'll be sorry."

"Yes," Jake agreed grimly, "We'll show him alright!"

Chapter 5

Jake didn't sleep well that night with the knowledge that his arch enemy was only metres away from him. Maisy couldn't understand the problem and why the brothers were constantly at war with each other, she had retreated to bed early that night, fed up with Jake's constant ranting. The dawn eventually came and with it so did Ben, who popped his head through the kitchen window with a plate full of bacon rolls. Maisy greeted him kindly and welcomed him in, offering him a freshly poured filter coffee. Jake wasn't too pleased to see him and immediately headed over to the farm, stopping only for a second to rev up mud all over Ben's pristine clean Ford. Maisy watched her husband splatter dirt with his motorbike into every direction imaginable, mud hit the kitchen window where she was washing the breakfast things.

"Don't worry. It'll wash." Ben reassured her, handing over his used cup and plate. "And while I'm at it, I'll wash your windows too."

"Thanks Ben. I can't understand why Jake is being so childish," said Maisy disgruntled, hanging up the damp tea-towel.

"He's always been a child. I'm making a roast on Sunday. Do you and Jake want to come over?"

"I'll ask Jake first, Sunday roast has always been his thing. Don't think he'll be too pleased to go to his brother's Sunday roast!"

"Let me know then. See you May."

As Ben left with a merry whistle, Maisy frowned to herself, why did Ben just call her May? That was Jake's name for her, nobody else knew that.

*

Ollie looked up from the hen coop as he heard Jake's motorbike pulling up, he silently prayed to himself, this wasn't going to be easy. He could see his farmhand's red face marching nearer and nearer towards him, it wasn't a pleasant sight and Ollie hoped there wouldn't be a fierce confrontation. Fortunately, Ben wasn't anywhere to be seen, he couldn't stand the strife between the two brothers.

"Ben moved in last night! What were you thinking?" Jake yelled, causing the chickens to scatter in alarm.

Ollie raised his eyes to the sky for a fleeting second, "He is my farmhand. And as you already know, I need my farmhand close by. In case something crops up or an emergency of sorts needs sorting out."

"I'm your farmhand! *Me!* Not him! What does he know about farming?"

"He's willing to learn. And he has proved himself useful. See for yourself, the farm is doing so much better now. The cows are milked, the chickens fed, the sheep are out to pasture. The fields are ploughed, the beans are sowed. And Ben has promised to fix up the main barn today and repaint it. What are you going to do today?"

"I'm…I'll be pumping out the water in the upper fields and laying down drainage to prevent future flooding."

"Ben already pumped out the water. Contractors have been to survey the land and we're waiting to hear back from them."

"Fine," Jake huffed, "I'll be fixing the combine harvester."

"Already done. I called a man in over the weekend."

"What shall I do then!?"

Ollie plumped himself down on the stone bench, rubbing his tired leg still bound in plaster cast, "How about…you take some leave? When was the last time you had a break? And Maisy is due soon, you don't want to miss the most important moment of your life."

Jake scratched his head with fatigue, Ollie had a point, he hadn't had a break for years now, the farm had always come first. He could finally take his wife away for a few days, she had always wanted to go to the Lake District, and he could finally get away from his brother too.

"Ok," Jake agreed. An emotion bubbled up in his stomach, something he hadn't felt for a long time…happy. To Ollie's surprise, Jake began to laugh and suddenly whooped with joy, "I want a month off, starting from now!"

"You got it," Ollie smiled, laughing with his farmhand, "And your job will still be here when you get back."

Jake raced back to Primrose Cottage, his heart pumped ecstatically as the blood rushed through his veins, giving him a rosy healthy glow to his cheeks. Maisy was surprised to see such a significant difference to Jake's mood change, she opened the door and stood dumbstruck,

"What's got into you?"

Jake guffawed and hugged Maisy, "Pack your bags. We're going to the Lake District!"

Maisy took a step back in alarm, "Now!? I'm due in two weeks Jake. I can't just go off like that. What if the baby comes?"

Jake suddenly felt deflated as he felt the happy feeling leave his body, "Why not May? It's only for a few days."

"I can't risk it, Jake. We should have gone before…not now. I'm sorry."

"Right. You're right." Jake sighed, dragging his sorry self into the house. "We'll go when the baby is old enough."

"Why don't you go by yourself? Or take a friend with you. Take Dan and Matt, make it into a fishing trip or something?"

Jake brightened up, "Ok. I'll sort something."

The following day Jake ventured into Whitehaven and visited the local fishing shop for some more tackle and fresh lines. The holiday was fully booked for himself and the lads, a proper lad's holiday with none of the wives joining them. A quick trip to the camping shop followed suit for some more gear, which he loaded into the back of Dan's car. Dan ran through the checklist twice; they were ready to go. The date for the holiday was booked for the following Monday after the Santa run, which they had promised Nick the publican that they would be there for. Daniel drove Jake home and they were surprised to find Constable Wright and a tall weedy looking fellow next to him. Dan hurriedly put the car into reverse, but it was too late, they were spotted. Constable James Wright, a skinny type of medium height, with large blue watery eyes sitting too close to his narrow nose, and brown short hair that flopped over his large ears. He waved them over and pointed to the gate outside Jake's house,

"Afternoon men. Step out of the vehicle please."

"What's this about Mr Erroneous?" Jake asked, clambering out of the car.

Constable Wright wasn't amused, having only been a bobby for a few years now, he found the Byrd family the most trying, "I've told you dozen of times. It's Constable Wright to you."

"Of course…Constable Wright. Can I help you?"

The weedy fellow stepped forward and coughed a hollow dry cough, "I'm Mr Connolly. I'm a forensic document examiner. Sign here for me would you sir?"

Jake took the clipboard from him and stared at the piece of paper confused, "It's blank. You want me to sign a blank piece of paper?"

"If you would?" The man suggested, clicking the top of his ballpen and handed it over to Jake.

"Why should Jake sign anything? Why do you need his signature?" Dan enquired, walking over to the small group, "What's going on?"

"It's for analysis. We need to compare your signature with another signature on a document. There's been talk of fraud." Constable Wright answered, addressing Jake.

"What document?"

"Sign the paper and we'll talk."

Jake sighed and took the pen, then unwillingly scribbled his trademark onto the page, "Now what?"

Mr Connolly wasted no time in extracting the clipboard from Jake's hand, pulled out a magnifying glass and precisely studied the page. Eventually he took out a document encased inside a punch pocket from his briefcase. He hawed and hummed for a minute then slightly nodded, "It's a match."

"What's a match? I have no time for these games!" Jake snapped, tossing the pen back to Mr Connolly.

"Your signature, it matches the one on this document," Constable Wright responded, beaming smugly for he finally had a hold over Jake, "Jake Byrd. I'm arresting you for illegally selling sheep that didn't belong to you, as a question of theft. You do not have to say anything, but it may harm your defence if you do not mention when questioned something which you later rely on in court. Anything you do say may be given in evidence. Do you understand?"

Jake growled angrily and his face reddened a bright tomato colour, "NO! I DO NOT BLOODY UNDERSTAND! I HAVEN'T DONE ANYTHING!"

"Jake…calm down!" Dan shouted at him, shaking him by the shoulders, "You'll only make it worse! Go with Mr Erroneous and I'll sort this out. GO!"

Constable Wright didn't look too pleased to be called Mr Erroneous again, but his mood brightened as he slapped the handcuffs onto Jake's wrists. He placed a hand on his head and guided him into the police car. Jake considered struggling but then decided against it, what was the point, he couldn't escape anywhere. Mr Connolly pulled a grim face at Dan, before driving off down the rutted road. Daniel ran his hands through his hair; what a dilemma! He realised there was only one person who could sort this out, Ollie. Without wasting another second, he ran across the fields toward Badgers Farm; the mud squelching and oozing past his ankles and covered his white trainers. Dan gave an irritable grunt, farming life was definitely not for him. To make matters worse, Ben was charging towards him in his little green tractor, the cultivator dragged behind noisily.

"Enjoying your walk?" Ben jeered, slowing down to a stop, "Need a lift?"

"Not from you I don't! Is Ollie about?" Dan called out, shielding his eyes from the sun as he looked up at the cabin.

"Ollie? Nah, he just left. Gone to see a farmer about some sheep or something? Don't know. He should be back soon though if you want to wait for him?"

Dan scowled at Ben, he knew that Ben was behind the rustling, but how was he going to prove it? A loud clatter of a truck and the sound of an engine roaring alerted Dan to Ollie's arrival at the farmhouse. Hurriedly Dan sauntered on, just as the farmer climbed out of the vehicle and disappeared into the house, the driver of the truck turned around and headed back up the lane.

"Ollie?" He called, panting from exhaustion, shocked at how unfit he was.

The farmer popped his head back out of the door, "Daniel? That you? Long time no see! Look…now's not a good time. Something has come up and…urgh. Come back tomorrow…yes?"

"I can't Ollie. It's about Jake. He's just been arrested for stealing sheep. But it's not true, he's been set up."

Ollie sighed as he yanked his tweed cap off, "Best come in then. Tea?"

Dan declined the tea, wandered through to the kitchen and drew out a chair, "Have the police been already?"

The farmer suddenly looked solemn and fatigued, "Yes. Apparently, Jake has stolen half of my herd of sheep, lambs too. I couldn't get up to the field to check, not with this leg busted. Carl, my neighbour, went up to the field this morning the moment we got told."

"Who's the buyer? Have you talked to him? What's going to happen now?" Dan persisted, twitching his leg in anticipation.

Ollie sat down next to him with his hot brew paired with two digestives, "Just come from there, Carl assisted me. Mark Hallum, over at Oakridge Farm. We go way back, he's not a very nice farmer, antsy I call it. Anyway, he's been looking to buy some sheep for a while now. Been after mine for years but I've always said no. Then my farmhand Jake, messages him out of the blue, offering fifty-six sheep and six lambs no less! Mark bought the animals straight up without question, but then he worried about the signature, he felt something was off. He came to me and showed me the electronic signature, I told him it must be a fake."

"Then Mark went to the police?"

"Must have done. I asked him to return my sheep, but obviously he wants his money back first. I was hoping to talk to Jake first, just unfortunate the police got there before me."

"You know it wasn't Jake…don't you? He's been your farmhand for more than fifteen years!"

Ollie shifted his body uncomfortably and rubbed his wrinkled forehead, "I don't know anymore. The police said the signatures fit almost to perfection."

"*Almost.* You just said *almost.* There's hope yet Ollie," Dan enthused leaping up, "I'm going to get him out of jail. Will you help?"

Ollie ignored Dan's enthusiasm and stared out of the window, shrugging his shoulders in defeat. But Dan wasn't defeated, there was hope, a small slither of hope, but it was there all the same.

*

Jake gloomily gazed unblinkingly at the wall opposite, his eyes traced the indented marks and graffiti from past prisoners. It was quiet in his cell…too quiet. No noise could be heard anywhere, the silence was driving him crazy. Suddenly there came a rattle of keys and a loud clink noise and the door swung open, banging into the wall with vigour.

"You can go." The police officer gruffly drawled, "You're released on bail."

"On bail?" Jake asked dumbfounded, "Who paid up?"

"I believe it was your brother. Jolly nice of him too…my brother would never do something like that."

Jake rudely snorted and stiffly stood up, "He was the git who got me in here in the first place."

"Well then, maybe he's just got a guilty conscience. Time to go Mr Byrd."

Jake ambled past the police officer and headed back up to the main desk, signed his release form and headed out. He was surprised to see a small congregation of people outside, Ollie, Daniel, Maisy, Ben and Ben's stupid friend Simon. A hubbub of voices shattered the silence, Jake rubbed his sore head with both hands, he could feel a migraine coming on. He walked over to Dan's car and leaned on the bonnet, Maisy walked over and joined him, leaving the men to converse amongst themselves.

"Everything ok Jake? Dan told me what's going on…tell me you had nothing to do with Mr Hart's sheep."

"I had nothing to do with Ollie's sheep. It was Ben…all of it was Ben." Jake grumbled tiredly.

"But why would Ben?"

"Yes…why would Ben do this? To land me in hot water, I guess. Make me lose my job."

"I'm sorry Jake, but Mr Hart has already come to a decision. We've been talking about it all day."

"Talking? Talking about what?"

Ollie sensed that the Byrd's were talking about him and limped over without the aid of a crutch, "Jake. I'm sorry Jake, I thought long and hard about this. I'm letting you go and replacing you with Ben. And…I want my money back…all of it if I'm to buy my sheep back. Also, I need the cottage back…as you know it comes with the job."

Jake felt like a great weight of bricks had just descended on him, knocking him down sideways into the tarmac. He felt like he had just been stabbed in the back. Everything began to spin and the voices around him became distorted. Maisy shook his arms, causing him to collapse further on the floor with shock.

"Why?" Jake whispered, wiping a tear from the corner of his eye, "I thought we were friends. I'm your best worker Ollie."

"*Were.*" Ollie corrected, "You *were* my best worker. But I can't have a dishonest one that steals from me. The idleness I turned a blind eye to, but this is one step too far. I'm sorry Jake."

Ben sensing his brother's anguish, wisely decided that now might be a good time to leave, he had no desire to provoke an angry and distraught lion. Simon followed after him back to town, he was a coward and secretly scared of Jake and his wild mood.

Maisy took her husband's hand, "I'll be at my sister's. Call me?"

Jake couldn't answer as he watched his wife climb into the Jeep, power up the engine and drive off into the night.

Dan patted him on the shoulder, "You can have my spare room for now. Till you figure out what you're going to do next."

Jake silently nodded, he knew what he was going to do next, he was going to get his job and home back.

Chapter 6

It was the noise of traffic the next morning that woke Jake, the beams from the headlights streamed across the ceiling. He wondered to himself how he managed to sleep through so much noise, it was such a vast contrast to the silence of the countryside. The time was nearly nine. On a normal day he would have been up hours ago, but he had to remind himself, it wasn't a normal day…far from it. Maisy hadn't called him; she must be doing ok. Jake pulled up his slipper socks and tugged down his pullover, it was cold in Dan's house and the radiators weren't on. The kitchen was even colder, it was like walking on ice as he gingerly stepped onto the tiles. Jake opened the fridge door and saw an empty space, apart from some milk and strange looking pâté. The cupboards were virtually bare, a few cans of essential baked beans sat next to the coffee and sugar.

"Beans on toast it is," said Jake silently, and opened a few more doors, "No bread. Beans it is."

There was nothing much to do at Dan's place, the television only had a few channels, and the radio was all static, and the only reading material were a few cook books. Jake sighed and curled up on the sofa with a blanket and browsed his phone. Dan walked through the front door an hour later, laden down with food shopping, "Morning. See you found something to eat. I'm not very good at stocking up on food. Izzy always saw to that."

Jake put down his cold coffee and helped unpack the bags, "What's with all the lager and crisps?"

"Man's got to eat and drink hasn't he?"

"What about bread and cereal?"

Dan grunted and ignored him, placing the last of the ready meals into the fridge, "Well we won't starve or die of thirst, isn't that the main thing?"

"I'll go and get some bread."

"Can you afford it?"

Jake turned to face Dan, puzzled and scared as to why his friend just asked that, "What do you mean?"

Daniel shrugged his shoulders nonchalantly, "You heard Ollie. He wants the money back so he can buy back his sheep."

"AND YOU THINK I SOLD THE SHEEP!? DO YOU!?" Jake raged, unnecessarily kicking the cold radiator, "IT WASN'T ME! I NEVER SOLD THE ANIMALS AND I HAVEN'T GOT THE MONEY!"

Dan puffed out a deep slow breath, "Well…Ollie wants the money back. One way or another. And…I can't see Ben paying up. He's probably spent all the money already."

Jake suddenly visualised Ben moving into Ivy Cottage, like Primrose Cottage it was part furnished, and yet Ben still had plenty of boxes as well as a sofa to move into his new home. Ben hadn't had a stable job in years and been claiming money from the government to act as their mother's carer, but the money was always spent quickly on mum and the house.

"Did Ollie ask how much he wants back," Jake demanded, flopping down on the armchair.

Dan cleared his throat a few times then dryly whispered, "£9440."

"£9440!" Jake exploded.

"Just, tell me you've got the money."

Jake gave a loud groan, he had the money in his life savings, what would Maisy say if he emptied out the account?

"Mr Erroneous will be stopping by later too," Dan continued, staring at the wall opposite, "He's given you twenty four hours to pay up or you'll receive a fine or worse…a short prison sentence for theft. You know I would offer the money if I had it, but I'm struggling enough as it is. I can't even afford heating! And on that note, I'm off to the gym for a hot shower. You coming?"

Receiving no response and knowing there was nothing left to say, Daniel grabbed a bag by the door and headed out. The gym was the crowning jewel to the little village of Whitehaven which only boasted a few charity shops, one café and the odd local business. Jake watched him leave from the window, the glass was so filthy he couldn't tell which side the dirt was on, he ran a finger along the side and wiped it on his trousers. Daniel wasn't a clean person, far from it. Jake found a hoover in the cupboard hidden under a thin layer of dust and proceeded to clean the floor at least. Once finished, he carefully stacked the dirty plates and bowls and placed them in the sink, there was plenty of time to wash up later. A knock came on the front door, a small quiet feminine tap. Jake leapt up from the sofa and burst open the door,

"Maisy! Oh…sorry."

Isabelle smiled shyly, "Hi Jake. I didn't know you were here. I'm actually looking for Dan."

"Dan isn't here," Jake stated and proceeded to close the front door. Isabelle looked deflated and Jake saw that she had been crying and his heart softened, "I'm sorry. That was cruel of me. You can come in and wait, he won't be long."

"I hope not, I've only got ten minutes. Joe is waiting for me in town, we're going shopping in Gresham and then tonight we're going dancing."

Jake offered a seat on the stained sofa and attempted to find some tea, "It's a right mess in here. I can't find the tea anywhere."

Isabelle opened the small cupboard door above the cooker, "Dan keeps his tea up here. I know…doesn't make sense, does it?"

"What did you want Dan for anyway?"

Isabelle shook her head and sat back down, "Doesn't matter. I'll talk to Dan when I see him."

"Ok. Here's your tea by the way."

"Thank you."

Jake nodded slightly and sat opposite her on a broken saggy armchair and eyed the clock on the side table. Isabelle noticed his direct eye contact and also kept a fixed gaze on the little alarm clock. The big hand ticked nearer and nearer to the twelve, Dan should be home soon.

"Well," said Jake and Isabelle in union.

"Yes," said Isabelle, picking up her coat, "I should be going."

Jake replied, "I'll let Dan know you called."

Izzy wasted no time in making a swift exit. Jake waited till she was well out of sight and made his way over to Dan's car, he couldn't wait any longer until his friend returned.

*

Primrose Cottage, once a house full of love and memories was now just a house. An almost empty house, apart from the main furnishings and white goods and the few odd farm pictures on the walls. Jake stepped over the threshold and was astounded at the stark difference, it was no longer home without his and Maisy's stuff in it. The walls were repainted white, and the paint fumes still lingered, even the carpets had been pulled up and replaced. Ollie certainly hadn't wasted any time, probably had help from Ben too no doubt. Jake headed outside into his garden, fortunately everything was still in place including the lean-to at the back. Slowly he ambled to the garage and nosed inside, nothing was touched or moved, and his bike was still there. Jake ran a loving hand over the frame and rubbed the handlebars, his pride and joy, now he just had to figure out where to temporarily keep his bike. Not at Dan's, too many bike thieves, maybe Maisy's sister would be happy to? With a sigh, Jake grabbed the cover and threw it over the machine, gave his bike a pat on the seat and closed the garage door. For a moment he stopped and stared across the fields to Badgers Farm, he felt sick with nostalgia and wondered, when did everything start going wrong? A rumble of a tractor could be heard in the distance; having no desire to bump into his brother, Jake departed. He would be back later tonight to converse with the farmer.

*

Daniel was home and had been waiting impatiently for Jake, he heard him forcefully open the stiff wooden door and then close it. Dan looked up from his armchair and grunted, "Where you been?"

Jake chortled and tossed his coat onto the stairs, "You sound like my wife! Just went up to the house for a final look. Suppose Ollie will be using it as a holiday lodge now, since Ivy Cottage is no longer available. Can you give me a lift up to the house later? My bike is still there, and I want to bring it back."

"Sure mate. Listen…I've been to see Mr Erroneous, he wants the money paid tonight. Apparently, the signature on the form is legit, Mr Connolly is a hundred percent certain it's yours. However, good news…the bank is willing to lend you a loan of ten thousand which you can pay back in instalments on a monthly basis."

"How is that good news? How am I supposed to pay back each month without a job?"

"Well…it's better than a fine or a prison sentence."

Jake gave in to his bestie, "True. And…thanks mate. Just remembered…Izzy came over."

"Izzy? What did she want? Is she ok?" Dan quizzed feeling worried and lit himself a cigarette.

"She'd been crying. She didn't say what she wanted. She only stayed fifteen minutes."

"She must have said something!" Dan demanded, puffing aggressively on his fag.

"Dunno…she mentioned shopping with Joe and then dancing in Gresham tonight."

Daniel leapt up and did a large clap with his hands, "This is it! We're going to Gresham and I'm going to bring back Izzy. I knew she wasn't happy with money boy, I knew it! There's only one place in Gresham for dancing and that's Murphy's."

"The mad Irish club full of Micks? You sure?"

"Positive."

"And what will Izzy say when we just happen to turn up?"

"She won't notice. It's a big place remember, it's got two floors. I know…how about your bring Maisy and I'll bring a girl I know and pretend to be on a date to make Izzy jealous.

Jake guffawed loudly and rubbed his temples, "You want me to bring my wife? My heavily pregnant female who might pop at any minute?"

Dan hummed and flopped back into his chair, "Yeah…that wouldn't work. And Izzy would be more angry than jealous if I brought another girl with me. How about we ask Matt and Phil? Lads night out."

"Lads night out? Where we just happen to walk into an Irish club? Right, I'm off to the bank. Actually, you can drop me off at Badgers Farm after the club. I'll use my bike to get back."

"Sure thing."

Jake grabbed his coat and walked out the door, narrowly missing a cyclist whizzing past on the pavement. It was well past lunchtime and Maisy still hadn't called, he pulled out his phone and hesitated over her name for a moment, then put his phone back. She would call if she needed him.

*

Night had closed in earlier than usual due to the thick cloud formation, snow gently trickled down and melted on the warm pavements. Jake waited impatiently for Matt and Phil to drive up, he was frozen to the bone and tired of sitting crouched and huddled up to the little heater in the living room. It was one thing being cold outside, you could just run around and get warm, but being cold inside was another thing. Jake liked his home comforts and being warm by a roaring fire, where you could stretch your legs and relax your body. Dan wasn't bothered by the cold in the slightest and lay sprawled out on the sofa under a thin blanket. A blast of a horn announced the boys arrival and Jake didn't waste a second getting his boots on and almost fell into the car. After a bit of banter, they drew straws, and declared Phil as the designated driver for the night and Matt slapped a badge onto his jacket. They arrived in Gresham in no time and within minutes they were out on the town, searching for their first port of call. Phil spotted a small nightlife place, they settled down and were quickly outnumbered by the amount of young people, so they headed out to a pub a bit further down the road. Jake couldn't help but reflect whether this was a good idea as their glasses got refilled for a third time, he was already feeling giddy and strange, and they weren't even at Murphy's yet. A large man in a leather jacket wearing shades approached them, there was a short scuffle and an exchange of angry words. Jake had no idea what was happening as they were escorted off the premises.

"Shall we head up to Murphy's now?" Dan asked and drunkenly sang, "Isabella is waiting. Isabella my queen!"

"Worst shanty in history," Phil joked, as he opened the door to the bar. An Irish band on stage were playing loudly with their varied Irish instruments, mostly strings which were plugged into the mains. Jake and Dan peered over the banister and watched the dancers dancing on the dance floor below, strobe lights flashed across the room lighting up the place temporarily.

"Look!" Dan shouted to his friends, "It's Isabella! IZZY! IZZY MY LOVE!"

Isabelle looked up to the balcony and shielded her eyes from the bright lights, she spotted Dan and his friends waving wildly and murmured, "Oh God."

Jake didn't wave to her, he was puzzled, "Who's she dancing with? Is that Joe?"

Dan focused his eyes in Jake's direction to see whom he was staring at and said, "That's not Joe. Is that? Is that Ben?"

The men grabbed their drinks, realising that Matt and Phil had already descended downstairs, and followed through after them. Isabelle politely hollered them over, giving them no choice but to obey. Jake wasn't happy about it, he didn't want to be seen talking with Ben. Ben seeing his brother approach, quickly made for the exit at the back of the club, he too had no desire to talk to his brother.

"Why are you here with Ben?" Daniel plunged in, accidentally clashing his drink with hers. "I thought you were on a date with Joseph?"

Isabelle suddenly looked sheepish and uncomfortably answered, "I am…sort of. I just bumped into Ben, and I recognised him. We got talking, had some drinks and danced. Joe wandered off somewhere, I don't know where he went."

Dan's face reddened, "I'm going to find him! Right now! He should know better than to leave his date on her own! What if something happened to you!?"

Isabelle grabbed his arm, "Dan. It's ok, I'm not on my own…not really. Dan!"

Dan ignored her and ploughed his way through the crowds, desperate to seek out his archnemesis. Jake eyed Izzy curiously, confused by her strange behaviour as she appeared fretful, and her breathing accelerated as she tugged on her scarf nervously.

"Joe's not here. Is he?" Jake suddenly asked. "You came with Ben. Is that what you going to tell Dan this morning?"

Isabelle cried, "Joe left yesterday morning to the Maldives with some girl, he left me a lying voicemail saying he's at a work meeting in Marsham and should be back tomorrow. I went to the local pub last night to look for Dan and I found Ben instead. Ben was really nice and kind, he said we should go to Murphy's, have a good time out and forget about everything."

"Nice and kind? Bet he was," Jake sulked to himself then said aloud, "So Joe lied to you about where he is. How did you find out?"

"You know that I work in a café? Well, there were some girls there talking and one of them said she was going to the Maldives with her boyfriend Joe Rogers. I brushed it off and told myself it was a coincidence. Till Joe rang and said an emergency meeting had come up." Izzy sobbed, accepting the tissue Jake handed to her, "I can't believe he lied to me."

"Seems like we're both having a bad week," Jake concluded desolately, swirling the liquor in his almost empty glass.

Isabelle squeezed his arm affectionately, "I saw you had moved in with Dan. What's happening?"

"Let me top up your glass and I'll tell you."

Chapter 7

Daniel had returned to the duo in a raging mood, not helped either by the amount of alcohol he had been drinking. Joe was nowhere to be seen and Dan concluded that he probably had already left. Jake wanted to tell him where Joe really was but decided not to make matters worse and he had made a solemn promise to Izzy to keep stum. It was nearly midnight by this point, and everyone knows from fairy tales that the magic ends at midnight, and the lads had enough for one night. Phil especially had enough, having only been allowed soft beverages to while away the time, and dancing wasn't his forte. However, Dan's mood quickly elated when Isabelle realised that she was without a ride and squeezed in next to him in the back of Phil's car. Just as they reached the outskirts of Whitehaven Jake patted his mate on the shoulder,

"Slow down Phil. Can you drop me off here?"

Phil obediently pulled over to the side laughing, "What here? You need a piddle or something?"

Jake ignored his crude sense of humour and slammed the car door shut, "Yeah sure. I'll find my own way back. Don't wait for me."

Phil was puzzled by Jake's strange behaviour, but he was too tired to argue or find out what was going on, and carefully drove off into the night with his fog lights on full. Jake didn't wait for them to leave and was already on the familiar track back to his house. It was dark inside the house, which usually wasn't the case. Jake had come home late many times, and there had always been a comforting glow from the lamp downstairs that Maisy would leave on for him. Quietly he grabbed the garage door handle and slowly pushed the door up, wincing as the door made a loud squeak on the rusted wheels. A light came on next door and Jake held his breath and swiftly ducked under the half open door and hid behind some old crates. He waited and watched the light on the road, not daring to move a muscle as an uncomfortable cramp tormented his leg. It seemed ages, but eventually the light turned off as Ben retreated back to bed. Jake wasted no more time and pushed the door up the rest of the way and made his way over to a mound by the wall and pulled the cover off.

"What the?" he exclaimed, forgetting to be quiet, "Where the hell is my bike!?"

Angrily he rummaged through the rest of the garage, pulling off the covers of other stored away items, his bike wasn't there. His trusty bike and after so much love and money lavished on it, all the memories and good times, stolen with the click of a finger.

"Ben!" Jake growled to himself and kicked the crates, "THAT'S IT! You've gone too far this time! Too far!"

Ben must have heard his older brother raging about in the garage, no lights came on and no noise was heard from Ivy Cottage. Jake pulled out his phone and called his friends, no one answered. Giving the crates a final kick, Jake stormed off back down the track. Fortunately, Dan's place was only on the other side of the village, an hours walk at most. Jake barged into his friend's house and slammed the door; he didn't feel well. The shock and the booze weren't a good mix and he found himself chundering in the toilet before passing out on the sofa. A while later something caused him to stir, and he felt a weight being thrown on top of him and warmth encircling his body. Jake opened an eye, pulled the electric blanket up to his chin and carried on sleeping. Dan watched his friend sympathetically for a moment whilst finishing off his breakfast, then made an effort to tidy up a little before heading out the door.

*

Isabelle was surprised to find Dan outside her house so early in the morning. She yawned and brushed the locks of hair away from her face, a smear of mascara blackened her hand as she rubbed her tired eyes,

"Dan? Do you know what time it is?"

"About nine last time I looked. I just wanted to see how you are? You know…after last night." Daniel replied and presented her with a bunch of flowers. "For you."

Izzy smiled gratefully and took the roses and smelt them, "Thanks Dan. Do you want coffee?"

"I wouldn't say no to a coffee."

"Okay, come on in then. Can you give me ten minutes to fix myself?"

Dan nodded and headed into the living room and flopped into the large saggy sofa that attempted to swallow him up. He loved being at Isabelle's place, it was warm and inviting with a feminine touch of flowers in each room, knick-knack's lined the shelves, and with a slight dusting of pink in the curtains. Mimi found him sitting in her spot and immediately jumped onto his lap, purring and head-butted his shoulder for attention. Dan lovingly stroked the cat's back, a pile of long dark brown hair stuck firmly onto his woolly jumper as he rubbed Mimi's ears. Isabelle finally returned with a pot of coffee and croissants, placed the vase of red roses in the centre of the table and invited Dan to join her. Mimi sensing that cuddle time was over, jumped down to the floor and began to wash her paws, Dan took the opportunity to sit down next to Isabelle.

Isabelle passed him a jammy croissant, "So…what's so important that it couldn't wait till later?"

Daniel hastily brushed the pastry flakes off his chin, "I only wanted to make sure you're ok. And…"

"And…?"

"And…to ask if everything's ok between you and Joe. By that I mean…what happened last night? I mean…why did Joe suddenly take off like that? What made him leave? Have you two broken up?"

Isabelle awkwardly shuffled in her chair, "More coffee?"

Dan looked at his full cup of coffee with confusion, "I've got plenty thank you. Are you going to explain what happened last night?"

"There's nothing to explain…trust me."

"Ok fine," Dan backed down, he knew better than to argue with his ex-girlfriend. After a minute he took a sip of exceedingly sour coffee, "How come Ben was there? Doesn't seem to be his kind of place."

Izzy groaned and smacked her hand on the table, "You don't stop…do you!? Who cares if Ben was there? The door is open for anyone to walk in."

"True. But isn't Ben more of a pub goer? He doesn't strike me as someone who goes to a club on a Saturday night."

"Well neither do you! When was the last time you went to a club? And last night doesn't count!" Isabelle almost screamed with frustration, "Great! And who is that knocking?"

Dan admired her angry walk as she strutted to the front door, pushing the chair in the hallway to one side with vigour. He heard her first whispering then shouting at someone which very quickly escalated into a heated argument. Quietly he sleuthed into the living room and peered through the netted curtains, not realising that Mimi had reclined to the windowsill and affectionately rubbed her face into his. The argument outside suddenly stopped and Dan knew he had been seen. Joseph strode into the living room with Isabelle on his tail and marched right up to him,

"Who are you and what are you doing in my girlfriend's house!?"

Dan was stumped and stuttered, "I'm just a friend of Izzy's. Just making sure she is ok after last night."

"Ok?" Joseph asked bewildered, taking a step back, "Why wouldn't she be, ok?"

"You left her on her own! Idiot! You left her by herself in the club, thankfully Ben was there to look after her."

"What club? And who's Ben? Listen here mate…I was away at a work meeting all day yesterday, I've only just got back this morning. Didn't Izzy tell you?"

"A 'work meeting'! Is that what we're calling it these days?" Isabelle snapped, stepping in between the boys. "You've just admitted just now that you went to the Maldives with some girl!"

"I already said I'm sorry!" Joe pleaded, reaching out to Izzy, "It's over between me and the girl, I promise you. I will never do it again."

Dan waved his hands about and addressed Izzy, "Whoa, hold up. You already *knew* that Joe was at this supposed work meeting slash Maldives? Why were you at Murphy's by yourself then? Oh…I see, you went with Ben."

Isabelle blushed bright crimson, "I was going to tell you yesterday morning. I went round to your house, but you were out. I saw Ben the night before and I told him that Joe was cheating on me. Ben felt sorry for me I guess and suggested we hit the town."

"Why didn't you say that then when I asked you last night where Joe was?"

"I don't know. I didn't want you to know I was out with Ben. You hate his guts and so does Jake."

"I'm so confused," Joe moaned, rubbing his head, "Why did you go to Dan's house then? Were you going to tell him about Ben, or weren't you?"

"I was going to tell Dan that you were cheating on me. I wanted Dan to go with me to Murphy's, not Ben." Isabelle mumbled quietly then grumpily swung back on Joe, "You need to leave. Go on. Get out! It's over between us Joe."

Joe opened his mouth to say something, but immediately shut it again when he saw Isabelle glaring at him irritably with piercing eyes. Silently he took his cue and dawdled sullenly out the front door.

Dan smirked, "That showed him! Poor money boy. Thinking he can buy my Izzy with money!"

"You should go too Dan." Izzy sighed and prompted by opening the front door again, "I know why you're really here and the answer is still the same. We're not getting back together, you're too needy and clingy. Move on, please."

"Izzy…I."

Isabelle ignored his plea and firmly closed the door, the rattle of a chain and a bolt being slid home was heard, no-one was getting back into the castle. Dan plonked himself on the top step, disgruntled and depressed that his Izzy had so aggressively shut him out. Joseph however hadn't left yet, and casually leaned onto his silver Mercedes, smoking an expensive looking cigar,

"I think I remember you now. You were at Ziggy's when we were there. You walked right past my table. It's Dan…right? I see what Izzy means now, she was saying how clingy and possessive you were. You can't let her go…can you? You actually stalked your ex to see who she's now dating."

"*Were* dating," Dan smugly stated, "She dumped you too, idiot."

"I might be an idiot, but look who's rolling in the money," Joe proudly replied with a big grin, "Aren't you still wearing the same shabby clothes from last week? Got your heating working yet?"

Dan's smug facial expression drooped, "It doesn't matter if I'm poor. I make Izzy happy, I treat her right, I look after her and I love her. Isn't that what matters?"

Joe snorted, "Anyone can have those qualities. Money is what matters. A girl wants a man who can give her a home, clothes, food, expensive holidays, more money than she can spend in a lifetime."

"At least I've never cheated on her."

Joseph growled irritably, "It was a mistake. I won't make that mistake twice. I will have Izzy back, she is *my* girl."

Daniel truculently retaliated, "Izzy has *always* been my girl. Ask anyone in the village!"

"Then let this be war. May the best hand win."

The men solemnly shook hands and Dan replied, "It's war."

*

Dan returned to his home in an elated mood despite the fact that Isabelle had evicted him from her home. Jake was still passed out on the sofa. Dan couldn't ask him for advice on what to do next. Various shouting could be heard from outside, a lorry had got stuck in the street and was having difficulty in reversing back down the little lane. Daniel breathed heavily on the glass and drew patterns into the mist, watching the few locals that had come out, signalling vigorously to the driver. Old Ernie gave a loud cry as the wingmirror from the lorry knocked down his hanging basket full of white pansies and ivy. As Dan watched the debacle, it suddenly dawned on him that Joe's house was just outside Whitehaven and there was only the one road to get into the village, he would have to drive past sooner or later. That beautiful shiny silver Mercedes with its flashy personalised numberplates, it would be a shame if something happened to it. Daniel grinned to himself and perched himself by the window, waiting for Joseph to drive past on his way back to Isabelle. And that's where Jake found him later, huddled up next to the windowsill with a blanket, eating a steamy ready meal with stringy cheese on top.

"Morning."

Dan turned to face him and nodded, "Afternoon."

Jake looked at the little clock and realised to his horror it was well past two in the afternoon, he hadn't meant to sleep in that long.

"You look well," Dan continued, turning to face out the window again. "You needed the sleep. There's a lasagne in the fridge if you want it?"

Jake shook his aching head, he needed a strong coffee after a visit to the lavatory. Later on, with his beverage in hand, Jake sat down and checked his phone. Maisy still hadn't called or even messaged, she must be busy. Dan still hadn't left his post.

Jake quizzed his friend, "What *are* you doing? You've been sat there for the past half hour!"

"Waiting for Joe."

"Of course…makes sense," Jake replied sarcastically from the kitchen, pulling the film off his pot of porridge and placed it in the microwave.

"Me and Joe are at war over Izzy. I'm waiting for him to drive past on his way to hers and then I'll mess up his car."

"Are you nuts!? We're not living in a fairy tale where two grown men fight like knights for the hand of the princess!"

"She's my princess Jake. You will never understand what I'll do for her." Dan mumbled silently, placing his finished meal down onto the little table.

"Whatever. I'm going down to see Mr Erroneous."

"I was thinking. Don't you think the whole thing is a bit strange? This Mr Connolly, showing up like that with Mr Erroneous and confirming on the spot that it's definitely your signature on the form. Don't they usually have forensic equipment or something to check properly? The magnifying glass is so old school."

Jake shrugged his shoulders as he pulled on his thin jacket, "We both know Ben is behind it. But even if we did prove it was him it won't change anything."

"What are you on about? If we can prove it was him, you'd get your job back, your house, your reputation and Ben will have to pay back the money not you. Trust me, it's near impossible to get a job when you've been fired. Oh crap, it's money boy! I got to go."

"Great, you can give me a lift into the village."

"Where's your ride? I thought you were bringing your bike back to mine?"

"Ben nicked it. Probably sold it too."

"God, I really hate your brother."

"Not as much as me. I could kill him right now."

Chapter 8

Jake scrambled out of the vehicle right next to the police station, he was barely out of the car when Dan sped off after his enemy just as the traffic light turned green. Dan followed the Mercedes down the crescent and grinned to himself for his prediction was spot on. Joe pulled up right in front of Isabelle's house and parked diagonally on her thin driveway, narrowly missing her prized garden gnome. He hauled out a large expensive bunch of flowers from the front passenger seat, slicked back his greasy hair and rang the doorbell excessively. After a moment Izzy forcefully opened the door and stood there for a second. Dan watched keenly from behind the neighbour's low hedge where he was hiding crouched down on the ground. He could hear Joseph pleading humbly, begging her to think twice and to give him another chance. Isabelle must have given in at that point, she held the door wide open and sullenly let him in and moodily shut the door. Dan saw his chance and didn't waste a second. He grabbed the can of paint from the boot of his car and snuck over to the back of the Mercedes. Stubbornly the lid wouldn't come off. Dan pulled out his large Stanley knife from his trouser pocket, unfolded it and ran the blade around the rim, eventually it popped off and paint splattered onto his jumper. He breathed in deeply and paused for a second. No-one was about and he could hear Joe and Izzy arguing inside. Like a flash of lightening, Dan donned the paint all over the Mercedes, orange paint oozed all over the sides and squelched into the crevices. Feeling rather smug and pleased with himself, he made a swift exit home. His work here was done.

*

It was well past nine at night when there came a knock on his front door, England was only seconds away from scoring their first goal, Sweden was still in the lead with two points. Half time was creeping closer, there was only fifteen seconds left on the clock, another foul tackle from Sweden. Daniel couldn't take his eyes off the game and impatiently called out,

"Door's open!"

"Mr Cooper?"

Dan jumped with surprise, he had been expecting his friend Jake to be entering the property, hurriedly he yanked the blanket off and greeted his visitor, "Mr Erroneous. Rather late to be calling, isn't it?"

Constable Wright glared at him, "I was actually on the way home. I'm here to give you this."

Daniel took the pieces of paper from him and quickly skimmed through it, "Don't get it. What's this for?"

"This," Constable James Wright began, feeling rather exasperated, "This is a restraining order to stay away from Isabelle Crow. You've damaged her property with paint and wielded a threatening weapon also on her property. You're not allowed to be within one hundred metres of her or you'll be arrested. Clear?"

"No. Nothing about this is clear at all. Who asked for a restraining order?"

"Mr Rogers. Isabelle's boyfriend."

"Ex-boyfriend actually." Dan retaliated crossly, "This is his revenge…isn't it!?"

"You damaged his car Mr Cooper and waved a large knife about, you vandalised Miss Crow's driveway with paint and broke her gnome, it's all recorded on the security camera. Mr Rogers and Miss Crow were scared for their lives. Apparently, you've been threatening them lately, they thought you were going to maim them or worse!"

Dan scoffed loudly and chuckled, "Tosh! It's all tosh! I used that knife to open the can of paint, I forgot to put it away, that's all. I wasn't going to use it to hurt someone. Joseph has been lying, can't you see that?

They were arguing inside, they didn't even know I was outside."

Constable Wright picked up his bicycle and saddled it, "The evidence doesn't lie Mr Cooper. Unless you want a court case…stay away from Isabelle."

"How much did he pay you?"

"What?"

"Joe. How much did he pay you?"

"Nothing. Nothing at all. Good night, Mr Cooper."

Daniel rudely slammed the door shut in the copper's face and tore the paper into miniscule pieces, "Prick! Must have been a handsome sum! Right…plan B."

*

Jake returned early the next morning and was surprised to find Dan up and ready, sitting at the kitchen table with a notepad and pen in hand. He had a faraway look in his eye and barely acknowledged the fact that his best friend had just walked in.

"Morning." Jake drawled, walking in with a yawn and flicked on the kettle.

"Ssh!" Dan retaliated aggressively and pointed to his phone, Jake immediately turned the kettle off and stared quizzingly at his friend.

Dan raised his index finger to hush his friend as someone on the other end picked up,

"Morning, this is British Gas. Emma speaking, how can I help?"

"Morning this is erm…Mark. Mark Rogers."

"Morning Mark, how can I help?"

"It's regarding my erm…late brother…Joseph Rogers. Sadly, he died over the weekend, and left me to deal with the house."

"I'm so sorry to hear that Mr Rogers." The lady soothed.

"Thank you," Dan replied, "I would like to stop the electric and gas please.

"Ok, shouldn't be a problem. Where does your brother Joseph live?"

"Whitehaven."

The clacking of a keyboard being tapped vigorously at speed could be heard, "Joseph Rogers of Whitehaven Point?"

"Yes, that's him."

"Ok. Give me ten minutes to sort that out for you."

Dan waited impatiently as he heard Emma on the other end tutting to herself, finally she confirmed that the services to the house had been cancelled. Dan did a small gleeful jig and hung up the phone,

"One point to me! That'll show him for sure! Now, time to call BT."

"Right," said Jake, scratching his head and pulled his boots back on. "I've got a few errands to run myself, possibly a new job in the next town over. Can I borrow your car?"

Daniel nodded his head and threw his car keys at him, "Here."

*

Damp rain drizzled down and an icy north wind picked up, Joseph zipped his luminescent green coat up higher to his chin and rubbed his gloved hands together. A quick glance at his Fitbit told him that it was nearly four, just enough time to get changed before taking Isabelle out for a second date. Whitehaven Point came into view, he fumbled about with his pockets and eventually produced a front door key.

"Hurry up Joe! It's freezing out here!"

"Ok Zoe! I'm doing it now."

Zoe groaned as Joe dropped the keys down the back of the large phormium wedged into a little stone plant pot. Night was settling in now and Joe struggled to feel for the keys, he pulled his gloves off and scrambled in the dirt, mud caked underneath his fingernails.

"God! Take me back to the Maldives," Zoe muttered under her breath, pulling her bright pink hood over her head.

"What was that?" Joe enquired, pulling the key out from its hiding place and unlocked the door.

Zoe ignored him and rudely pushed past, sighing with relief as the warmth from the hallway radiated her whole body, "I'm going to have a shower. My body hurts after that long run!"

"If you can call it a run," Joseph mumbled, pushing his shoes into the shoe rack, "More like a lazy jog!"

Fortunately, the girl didn't hear him and was already on route to the bathroom, the steam from the shower was hot and inviting. Joe immediately headed to the kitchen for a protein shake, the sound of the blender filled the kitchen with an ear deafening roar. He closed his eyes and imagined for a second, he was back in the Maldives, the white sand and warm seas, tropical palm trees swaying in a gentle breeze, locals handing out sweet pineapples on a stick. Something was calling him back to reality, a whining and whinging voice. Joe reluctantly opened his eyes and was startled to see Zoe wrapped in a towel with shampoo dripping from her hair, she shouted at him over the noise from the other side of the kitchen,

"Your hot water stopped working Joe! I can't finish my shower! Sort it out will you!"

Joseph laughed as she huffily retreated back upstairs; turning off the blender, he made his way to the utility room and checked the boiler. The little blue flame had gone out, crossly he hit the panel and flicked the switch a few times but with no result. He picked up his phone to call the energy company but all he could hear was an endless long beep, the phone line was out. Joe picked up his mobile, no signal. Suddenly the lights flickered out descending the kitchen into darkness and silence as the blender ceased its roaring. Rummaging through the top drawer, he found a pocket torch and flicked it on. Picking up on two glaring eyes from the hallway he yelped with fear and promptly dropped the torch,

"Blummin' heck Zoe! You scared the daylights out of me!"

"The lights have gone out! How can I finish my hair now? And your house is getting colder by the minute!"

"Everything is fine Zoe. I'm sorting it out now, give me a moment to put a fire on…ok?"

"NO! It's not ok! Why haven't you been paying your gas and electric bills? I thought you were filthy rich? You're obviously not, that's plain to see! Are you broke? You are…aren't you? I knew it! Is this even your house or are you just pretending? You know what…forget it, I'm going home."

After quickly changing back into her daywear, she grabbed her sports bag in the hallway and stormed out of Joe's house, her wet hair still tightly bundled in a towel. Joseph watched with amusement as she climbed into her 4x4 and revved with speed down the driveway, the little red tail lights soon vanished into the night. Whistling quietly to himself, Joseph headed back inside to build a fire, the cold was closing in now uninvitingly. He knew who was behind this farce,

"Daniel Cooper. You clever man," Joseph chuckled quietly to himself and poured his shake into a tall glass, "You might have won this round, but no-one messes with *my* house. No-one."

*

Jake suddenly awoke in alarm, his heart raced and beat painfully against his ribs, it was almost eight in the morning. What had woken him? Was it a nightmare, he couldn't remember. He heard the sound of a van from outside his window, cautiously he opened the curtain to take a peek. It was still too dark to see what make of vehicle it was, but the bright headlights lit up the front garden luminously. There came a shuffling noise in the hallway and the sound of a chair being knocked over. Jake craned his head round the bedroom door and squinted his eyes down the stairs; straining his ears as hard as possible as he could hear voices. A burly, bald man headed up the stairs, his large frame filled up the space. Upon seeing Jake, he grunted,

"Morning."

Jake nodded at him and returned to his bed, whatever Dan had planned he didn't want to be a part of it.

The man walked into the bedroom like he owned the place and roughly poked Jake in the back, "Oi! You can't sleep here mate. We need everyone out."

Jake rolled over and scowled at him, "Why?"

"We're shutting this place down. If everything is given the all clear, you can move back in."

"What do you mean if everything is given the all clear? Is there a bomb hidden somewhere or a terrorist hiding?"

The man guffawed loudly and held his belly, "Nah. Rats. There are reports of vermin in the property. We need to inspect every nook and cranny and get them critters out."

Jake grumbled irritably and clambered out of his warm sheets, "Fine! Let me get changed first. Where's Dan? I want a word with him."

Daniel was outside clasping a hot cup of Costa coffee between his hands and noticing his friend's stormy arrival passed Jake a cup from the tray. Two more men wearing hard hats strode past carrying equipment, one of them pinned a sign to the front door saying Do Not Enter. With the sun now coming up Jake could finally read the company name on the side of the van, Hey Pest-O, Pest Control Services.

"Why is pest control here? We haven't got any pests!" Jake aggressively questioned, moving away from the path as another man waltzed past.

Dan infuriatingly shrugged his shoulders and took a long sip, "It's not my doing. It's payback."

"Payback? For what? Oh god…Joseph is behind this. I'm right…aren't I?"

"Looks like it. It shouldn't take too long, once they've seen there's no vermin on the property they'll be on their way. Joe won't win this round easily."

Jake slammed his cup down on the tray, upsetting the contents everywhere, "You're maddening! You know that!? I'll be with my wife, I've been offered a new job in Slapton. We're going to look at houses today."

Dan appeared surprised, "You didn't say you had a new job. That's good news I suppose. Do you have the funds for a deposit?"

Jake glumly nodded, "Fortunately I still have just enough. Maisy doesn't know yet that we have no more money in the savings though. I paid Ollie back every penny."

"It's ok, I won't tell Maisy, mum's the word. I still don't think it's right that you coughed up the money."

"Yes well. I don't want to go to prison. I figured that once we get Ben to confess, he can pay me back the money instead."

Dan pulled out a pack of cigarettes from his pocket, "Your call mate. If that was me, I wouldn't let my brother walk all over me. I would have beaten the truth out of him."

"Yeah, like that definitely wouldn't land me in a cell," Jake responded sarcastically, "Ok I'm off, got a bus to catch."

"Sod the bus, I'll give you a lift. It's not far to Maisy's sister, is it? I need to warm up in the car anyway, it's like the Artic out here."

*

Ziggy's Pizzeria was full to the brim of contented diners, a long queue formed outside the door and into the street. The snow had picked up in size and pace, large snowflakes gracefully swirled and descended down onto the road. A few of the queuers found the extreme weather conditions too much and gave up attempting to secure a place in the little restaurant. Daniel had been waiting and watching for nearly an hour now, his bare hands were red and sore, and the tips of his fingers were almost blue. He had successfully followed Joe and his date to Gresham, his phone was poised and ready for action; it was just unfortunate really that he couldn't get a good photo, if only they were a bit nearer. He could see the girl throw her head back in merriment, clutching her heart and wiping away another loose tear. She was a beauty with her long dark hair that coiled across her strapless dress, but she was nothing compared to Isabelle. Dan watched as Joe reached over the table and stroked her hand, the girl responded by leaning across and kissed Joe fondly. Eventually they stood up and he could see the girl wriggling her arms into a thin fur coat, Joe had disappeared from sight.

"You're back, are you?"

Daniel leapt with shock and relieved within seconds that it was only the waitress from before, he managed to stutter, "Hi yes. Right. I'm…waiting for a friend."

"Would that be the same friend from last time? He's here and you're here watching him again, bit of a funny coincidence…don't you think?" The waitress drawled in a Mediterranean accent, stamping out her fag.

"Not really," Dan replied, silently begging his brain to come up with a quick answer, "A friend waiting for a friend."

"Hmm. Ok…I'll let your friend know, they're just about to leave now."

"NO! Wait…I!"

The waitress had already turned sharply on her heels through the back entrance of the restaurant. Dan cursed out loud, causing the people queuing to give him a hard stare. Then suddenly a piece of good luck came his way, Joe had returned from the toilets and was giving the girl another snog right in full view this time. Daniel didn't hesitate and immediately took photo after photo of the couple; triumphantly he flicked through the pictures on his phone. A voice suddenly boomed behind him,

"Give me the phone and no-one gets hurt."

Dan quickly wheeled round, only to see Joe standing in front of him with his fists clenched and ready, Daniel couldn't help but laugh, "What are you going to do? Hit me?"

"If I have to. The phone…now." Joe growled, holding out his hand. The girl looked terrified and tried to pull Joe away, but he rudely shrugged her off and elbowed her in the ribs.

"No," Dan replied haughtily, "It's my phone. Wait till I show Izzy that you're still cheating on her."

"What's he on about Joe?" The girl stammered, her whole body shaking from the cold as she wrapped her thin shawl tighter round her shoulders.

"Nothing Zoe," Joe answered and held out his keys, "Go wait in the car, I won't be a second."

Zoe obediently did as she was told, she had no desire to argue or wait any longer in the cold.

Dan sneered, "I hope that Zoe will leave you, now that she knows you're a cheat. And Isabelle will never get back with you either, once she sees the photos you're done for."

Joe laughed evilly and clicked his knuckles, "How will you do that? You have a restraining order in place my friend, you're not allowed to contact her or go near her."

"I'll send them to Jake then. He can show her the photos."

"Oh? Are you friends with Jake Byrd? What a funny coincidence. Well, he won't pass on the photos, if he does…I'll make sure he gets fired."

"What you on about?" Dan asked bewildered and worried, "He's already been fired from the farm."

"He's been fired already from a job?" Joseph pondered, stroking his beard, "That's news to me. Jake is working at Slapton High School as a cleaner. I hired him. Or did you forget that I'm the headteacher there?"

Dan's face paled, Joe took the opportunity to gloat even further, "Unless you want your little friend to get fired again, I suggest you delete those photos right now."

Daniel snarled and moaned to himself for a moment, then unwillingly deleted the photos and showed Joe they had vanished for good.

"Not so hard, was it? Now excuse me but Zoe is waiting for me."

"You're scum. You know that!? SCUM! Wait till I tell Isabelle what a horrible creature you are!"

"Tut-tut. Restraining order my friend."

"I'm not your friend!"

Joe didn't hear him, he was bracing himself headfirst into the snowstorm that had picked up, the streets were silent now and Ziggy's Pizzeria had closed for the evening. Dan paced frustratedly up and down the pavement, why didn't Jake say he was working for Joe? How was he going to prove to Isabelle that Joe was still cheating? One thing was certain, there was no way on earth that he was going to let Joe have his girl. One way or another, Isabelle would come back to him and him only.

Chapter 9

Dan propped himself on a bar stool, hurriedly he scoffed down the last of the cornflakes, time was ticking, and he was already late. Gulping down the last dregs of his coffee he grabbed his coat and ran out of the door, almost forgetting his keys and wallet in the process. Half the village had turned up for the big event of the year, the early birds had congregated in The Fox and Rabbit whilst the late arrivals hovered outside in the front garden. Pushing past the locals, Dan made his way over to the snug where Jake was based, handing out various sized Santa costumes.

"You're late!" Jake exclaimed, handing his friend a large outfit.

Dan jumped into his costume and tugged on the fake beard and donned his Santa hat, "Only by a few minutes. Has it started yet?"

Jake shook his head and adjusted his Santa cloak, "Obviously not, we're still here, aren't we?"

"Oh yeah. Sorry, stupid question. What time are we starting?"

"Half eleven. Turns out you're not the only one who's late. A lot of the villagers only turned up a minute ago." Jake chuckled merrily.

"Keep that up and you'll sound like the real Santa," Nick the publican joked, walking through into the little room and removed a pillow from under his shirt and sighed, "That's better. Being Santa is hard work! Are we ready to go Jake?"

"Ready." Jake responded enthusiastically.

"Great! Let's do this."

Nick's wife Jackie appeared nervous as she took centre stage, "Welcome everyone to our annual Santa Dash. Thank you for being here. As you know, it has been thirteen years since we lost our little boy George, he would have been twenty-one this year, same as his best friend Harvey. Thank you for your support, all moneys raised will go towards St Heliers Hospital."

There came a round of applause of admiration throughout the pub, followed by the slow departure as people filed out of the door. Nick had already run on ahead and was waiting attentively for the villagers to line up along the starting line. Jake and Dan aimed for the middle and were deeply amused to be surrounded by so many Santa Clauses. There were Santas to the left, right, in front and behind. A few women were dressed as Mrs Claus in stockings, while a few children had turned up dressed as elves.

"Think you're going to beat me, do you?" A mocking voice called through the crowd.

Jake turned to face his younger brother and barked, "It's not a proper race. It's a charity *fun* run you dope."

Ben pulled his older brother to one side so he could nastily whisper, "It might be a fun run to you brother, but…if you win this race…I'll confess it was me who sold them sheep. But if *I* win, it'll be you doing the confessing."

Jake couldn't restrain himself any longer, clenching his fist he swung it down, right into Ben's smug face where he stood. Ben immediately fell down clutching his nose and screamed in pain, Jake took the opportunity to throw in a few more punches. Ben's friend Simon and Daniel quickly held him back, Nick intervened and lead Jake away from the group.

"Oh, I'm hurt! I'm hurt really badly!" Ben cried out, holding his bloody nose. Isabelle hearing the commotion pushed past and knelt down next to Ben, dabbing his nose with a serviette she had brought with her.

"It's ok Ben," she soothed, stroking his hair, "It's just a bloody nose, it's not broken."

Some of the villagers were looking on, wondering what all the noise was about, Daniel cleared his throat loudly, "Shall we start this race then? It's getting colder by the minute!"

"What's the hurry Dan? You should be used to the cold considering you actually live in a freezer." Joseph quipped, sidling up to Isabelle and helped her back up as her long dress was restricting her movements.

"I don't think Isabelle wants you near her after last night!" Dan retaliated angrily.

"What happened last night?" Isabelle demanded, looking from Dan to Joe and back again.

"Nothing." Joe replied casually and smirked at Dan, "It's not worth losing one's job over, is it?"

Isabelle was thoroughly confused and turned to Dan for answers, but he refused to enlighten her and turned away. Nick had finally returned and held up a white flag,

"THREE…TWO…ONE…GO!"

One by one the locals began to run, jog and walk, there was much delight amongst them, and the sound of laughter could be heard throughout the village of Whitehaven. Ben was still lolling on the floor, Jake seized his moment and ran as fast as his could, taking everyone by surprise as he whooshed past. Joseph was an experienced runner, and he too ran on ahead. Dan hung back with Isabelle and noticed Zoe was slowly catching up to Joe. Joe pretended not to notice her, but Daniel wasn't fooled, unfortunately there was nothing he could do about it either, he couldn't risk getting his best friend fired. Ben eventually joined the run and was surprisingly athletic considering he wasn't the skinniest of people and managed to overtake the walkers at the back of the pack.

The end was in sight for Jake as he came round the last house in the village, it was just a matter of reaching the end of the road where the pub was situated. His Santa suit clung uncomfortably to his body and chafed in all the wrong places, but his determination powered him on. Nearing the hilly dip in the road, a big Santa figure suddenly appeared up ahead. Jake was confused and surprised, he thought he had overtaken everybody. The person was nearing the finish line, Jackie was cheering him on as he tore the red tape with his large frame and did a triumphant cheer with his arms. Jake almost tripped over with shock, Ben was jumping up and down in front of him with his arms raised, whooping with delight.

"YOU CHEAT! YOU CHEATED!" Jake rasped and panted with exertion.

Jackie quickly cut in and frowned at both of the men, "Enough! This is supposed to be a charity fun run.

Who cares if Ben won? You won last year Jake and the year before that."

Joseph and Zoe approached the finish line flushed and rosy cheeked, Dan and Isabelle caught up a short time later both thoroughly out of breath.

Jake however was still raging on, wiping perspiration from his forehead where his Santa wig clung on tightly, "Ben can't be a winner! He cheated! Look everyone…he hasn't even broken a sweat!"

Joe breathed heavily as he clapped Ben on the back, "Well done mate! I'll buy you a drink."

"Hang on! Does no-one actually care that Ben cheated here!?" Daniel demanded, removing his beard and hat and joined the huddle, "Jake's right…Ben's not even sweating or out of breath! That's not physically possible!"

"Don't be such a sore loser Dan. Maybe if you trained harder *you* might even win." Joseph retaliated, watching Zoe and Isabelle with interest as they walked into the pub together.

"I'm not upset that *I* lost. I'm upset because Ben cheated!"

Joseph pulled Daniel to one side to talk earnestly into his ear, "Look Dan, you're just one of life's losers. Not only have you lost this race, but you've lost the love of your life. You're a loser at your job. You've no money. Your home…if you can call it a home…is barely functioning. Your only friend is Jake, but only out of sympathy. Face the facts mate. You're a loser."

Daniel trembled, his eyes watered, and his heavy heart sank to the bottom of his stomach like a stone. Joe patted him on the back and headed into The Fox and Rabbit.

Dan felt downcast and trodden, then he perked up as he remembered something important and patted his pocket, "Loser? I'll show him who's the real loser."

The pub was completely packed out, Nick had disappeared and re-emerged with a sack of presents to hand out to the children. Jake had bought a round of drinks for himself, Dan, Joseph, Izzy and her new friend Zoe, deliberately omitting his brother and Simon. The atmosphere was tense amongst the small group, some of the locals sensing another fight on the horizon quickly dispersed back to the safety of their homes. Nick and Jackie were thoroughly drained, it was a big ordeal for them to host the Santa run in memory of their lost son, they piled the chairs up and began to clear up the place. The snowstorm outside was picking up in ferocity and the clouds grew darker. Jake and Daniel after having a few to many made their way to the toilets. Isabelle and Zoe not wanting to be with Jake's brother Ben, Simon or Joseph, grabbed their drinks and headed to the snug. For a moment there was peace in the pub, then suddenly the lights went out.

Nick shouted out to his customers to reassure them, "Circuits gone out again folks. Nothing to worry about. I'll just go…"

A horrific speedy explosion sounded, with glass shards shattering and scattering, followed immediately by an exact repetition, which deafened the end of his sentence. The girls screamed in fear and ducked under the table. Others copied their behaviour, but some stood frozen in terror. Only seconds later an eerie silence resounded throughout the place. Nobody dared move a muscle or dared to talk. A woman began to sob silently to herself and buried her head into her folded arms. Nick cautiously made his way to the bar and rummaged about for a torch. Jake and Daniel hearing the commotion rushed back in, stumbling over chairs that had fallen in the disturbance.

"Dan? DAN!"

Dan didn't waste a moment and rushed to Isabelle's side and wrapped her tightly in his arms, "It's ok Izzy. I'm here."

Isabelle buried her head into his chest, enjoying the comforting familiarity, quietly she whispered, "I'm so scared Dan."

"Where's Joe?" Zoe asked crawling out and held onto Isabelle's hand, "Damn it's so dark in here. I can barely see a thing! Is that Joe over there?"

"Sorry," Jake apologised. "It's only me."

Zoe glanced at Jake and suddenly let out an ear splitting shriek, Jake leapt with alarm then turned sharply to stare in the direction that Zoe was pointing.

"Oh, sweet God," Daniel whispered and stealthily made his way to the bar. Two huddled bodies lay sandwiched between the bar stools, blood oozed around their lifeless bodies. Careful not to step in the runny liquid, Dan felt for a pulse, their necks were still warm to the touch.

"Are they…?" Zoe began and sobbed.

The lights unexpectantly came back on and all hell broke loose, women screamed, and men shouted for answers. Chairs were knocked over in the turmoil and tables were aggressively pushed to one side as people aimed quickly for the exit. Nick casually returned from turning on the power supply and walked right into the middle of the hullabaloo. Noticing the dead bodies, he quickly took action and pushed the remaining few people into the snug and firmly closed the door, instructing his wife not to let anyone in or out.

"Call the police! Call an ambulance!" He commanded, staring at Jake and Dan who were still lingering by the bar.

Jake hurriedly grabbed the phone and called the local constabulary, informing them of the situation in hand. Daniel continued to stare at the bodies shocked and numbed, with a terrible sick feeling in the pit of his stomach. Nick patted him on the shoulder,

"I'll fix you both a brandy and we'll wait in the backroom for Constable Wright."

Jake and Daniel felt like there were in some sort or sordid nightmare, it took all their strength just to nod and follow through into the back. Nick rattled with the glasses and unsteadily poured a dribble into each glass, the three men looked at each other as they swung back the burning liquid. It was ten minutes later until the sound of sirens could be heard in the distance followed by the loud crunching of car tyres on salted gravel. Nick rushed to the entrance to let the policeman in,

"In here Constable Wright."

Constable James Wright calmly walked in with a very superior look about him, then seeing the messy state of the dead men, he promptly threw up in a corner. Dabbing his face with a handkerchief he profusely apologised and pulled out his notebook, "So sorry about that. Very unprofessional of me. Now then…can you run through today's events for me please."

"Do you want to check the bodies first?"

"Not really. Can't stand blood. Can you give me their names and I'll write it down."

"Ben Byrd and Joseph Rogers. Is the ambulance on its way?" Nick demanded, taking the young constable to one corner.

James Wright nodded, "Of course it is, shouldn't be too long."

"Right…well…I'm going to cover the bodies up. If that's ok with you? And then would you like to assess the scene of the crime first?"

"Sure…I can do that." Constable Wright amicably agreed and wandered through to the heart of The Fox and Rabbit, "What happened to the window? It's broken."

Nick frustratedly sighed, he wasn't happy dealing with such an unexperienced police officer, "The lights went out, we all heard gunfire and glass shattering. My guess is the bullets were shot through the window."

"How many shots were heard?"

"Two."

"What time?"

"3.30pm approximately. It was our Santa run today in memory of George…"

"Oh yes! I was going to take part but unfortunately, I was on duty."

"Yes…anyway. The run took part at just after 11.30am, people started to return about 12.30pm. A lot of people stayed for lunch, we put some sandwiches and savouries out on the table. About 3pm people started to leave for home."

"So…coming back to the men. Did anyone have any reason to kill them?"

"Talk to Jake Byrd and Daniel Cooper. There were 'words' between them right before the race, very ugly 'words' indeed." Nick explained, leading Constable Wright to the snug, "The rest of the witnesses are in here, if you have any more questions that is. Jake and Dan are in the back."

"Right," James Wright cleared his throat importantly, "You want me to talk to everyone else? Sure…I can do that."

Nick opened the snug door for him, and the rest of the party immediately jumped on him demanding answers, Constable Wright was soon quickly swallowed up into the throng. Jake and Dan hearing the raised voices emerged from their hiding spot and poured themselves another brandy from behind the bar.

"What a mess." Jake mumbled, taking a large sip and coughed.

"What a mess," Dan repeated, placing his empty glass down, "The worst part is…I couldn't care less that Joseph is dead or Ben. I'm actually relieved. Are you?"

Jake pondered for a moment then reluctantly nodded, "Yes, I'm extremely relieved. Sounds awful, doesn't it?"

Shouting and furniture being pushed around sounded from the snug, a short chubby woman with red hair and dark brown roots showing, pushed past the small mass of people blocking the exit. Breathlessly she marched right up to Dan and pointed a fat finger at his face,

"That's him officer. That's Dylan Worthy and he murdered my girl. He killed those men and I'll testify in court if I have to!"

The whole pub went silent, everyone gawped. No-one took their eyes of Daniel. Constable Wright nervously pulled out his rubber truncheon and handcuffs with shaking hands, "Daniel Cooper…or Dylan…whoever you are. I'm arresting you for the murder of Ben Byrd and Joseph Rogers. You do not have to say anything, but it may harm your defence if you do not mention when questioned something which you later rely on in court. Anything you do say may be given in evidence. Do you understand?"

"What!?" Jake exploded, "You can't just arrest him like that!? Where's the evidence!?"

"Search his pockets!" The chubby woman cried out.

Constable James Wright took a deep breath then slapped handcuffs on Daniel, who had obligingly put his wrists out for him, then searched through Dan's large Santa pockets. The young constable suddenly cried out and dropped something heavy on the floor,

"Ahh!"

"God. I don't believe it." Nick silently mumbled, using a napkin to pick up the gun from where it had fallen. "Dan? How could you?"

"Dan?" Isabelle sobbed and silently whimpered, "Tell me it wasn't you."

Daniel's face reddened but he kept his chin up, "It's Dylan. My name is Dylan. And no…I didn't kill Lisa or Harry and I didn't kill Ben or Joe."

Jake stumbled backwards and just caught himself from falling, "What you on about Dan?"

Daniel didn't reply and let Constable Wright lead him to his police car, humbly he bowed his head as he was lowered into the rear seat. Everyone watched from the window as the sirens came on and Daniel Cooper was taken away, no one knew what to say or think. Margaret Taylor grinned openly to herself, revenge was so sweet and satisfactory.

Part Two

Chapter 10

"Here. Have you read today's paper? That Worthy guy is on trial today, hope he gets sent down to rot in prison. You should have a read, it's all over the front page. Weren't you in charge of the Worthy case five years ago?"

Shutting my eyes thoughtfully I inhaled deeply for I remembered the Worthy case very well for its unsatisfactory outcome.

"Anyway," Sergeant Matthew Brody continued, "Boss wants to speak to you in ten. I'm off to visit that eccentric couple about their stolen fence."

I opened my eyes briefly as my sergeant flung the daily paper in front of my nose, a photo of Dylan Worthy took up most of the page with the caption, WORTHY TRIAL BEGINS. Squeezed into a side column was a description of the events that led up to his trial, Dylan Worthy would most likely spend life behind bars. I skimmed through the most part, but not wanting to keep the boss waiting I pushed myself up from my reclining position and headed upstairs. Cautiously I rapped on the door and a loud voice replied,

"Come in Jones. Have a seat."

I immediately sat down and watched the superintendent finish a very neatly written report with long curling letters. Clicking his ballpen and throwing it down, he finally addressed me,

"Jones. You know why you're here?"

I didn't have a clue, but I didn't want a long boring explanation either, so I simply replied, "Yes sir."

"Good. Good. What did you think when you heard about Worthy being arrested again and up for trial? Personally, I'm not convinced. The whole thing was a complete shamble from beginning to end. You were part of the Worthy case from the beginning, weren't you? It makes sense does it not, if you went to Whitehaven to sort this mess out and clean it up."

"Whitehaven sir? Where's that?"

"A small village the other side of Gresham."

"Gresham!? That's more than seventy miles away!"

"I know. You'll be staying at the local pub, The Fox and Rabbit. Pack your things, I want you there first thing in the morning." The superintendent concluded and returned to his writing.

Knowing that the meeting was officially over, I headed out and back to my little office and began to rummage through my files. Why all the fuss for an open and shut case? Dylan Worthy was the prime suspect for the first crime and the second, there's no such thing as coincidence, he was a murderer all right. I could still picture his face, those cruel blue eyes and hollow cheeks covered in uneven stubble; dirty hands and broken fingernails that shook as he lit yet another cigarette. I shuddered and pulled out the folder which was filed under 'W' and tossed it onto my table and slowly began to read:

Dylan Worthy age 33, a resident of St Heliers, has been arrested today (Saturday 14th October 2017) for the murders of Lisa Taylor age 29 and Harry Lucas age 29.

The events that are to follow started that Friday 13th October 2017 in the evening at 5pm. Dylan Worthy and his friends Nathan Marks, Lisa Taylor and Harry Lucas were out celebrating Nathan Marks 30th birthday at The Horse and Jockey by the sea front. They had some food and made their way to Sainsburys, by the marina, it's 7.30pm now. CCTV caught Dylan and Harry arguing and Dylan pushing Harry over, Lisa intervenes and pulls Harry back up. By 8pm they've made their way to Harry's boat, Maid of Splendour, the boat belongs to his parents. 10pm, a neighbour calls the police to report a disturbance of the peace, loud music is playing from the Maid of Splendour. Police turn up at 10.30pm and request the noise to be turned down, Nathan Marks leaves the boat. 10.45pm the police leave the area and head back to St Heliers police station. 10.49pm, the boat is seen on CCTV leaving the marina and heading out to sea. 11.17pm, CCTV footage shows the Maid of Splendour catching fire. 11.38pm, police, ambulance and RNLI turn up and attempt a rescue operation. 12.06am, Dylan Worthy is rescued from a dinghy and taken to hospital for minor burns. 12.32am, the fire is put out and the boat is brought back to the marina. 12.43am Lisa Taylor and Harry Lucas are *pronounced dead from third degree burns and smoke inhalation.*

Forensic evidence shows that the cabin-door had been latched shut from the outside. Harry, Lisa and Dylan were highly intoxicated at the time of event. The fire is believed to have started from a candle, there were many candles below deck and on top deck. Further evidence revealed that Lisa Taylor was Dylan Worthy's girlfriend before she started dating Harry Lucas.

The rest of the folder contained forensic reports, reports from the scene of the crime, witness statements and other bits of paper, nothing of interest there. Yet all the evidence pooled together pointed to Dylan Worthy as guilty. It was so blatantly obvious that he was guilty of what had been dubbed as, The Marina Murders. Why then did his super want him to look into the matter? Why did the jury unanimously vote, not guilty? Perhaps the answers were to be found in Whitehaven. Was Dylan Worthy guilty of the Whitehaven murders too?

*

Early spring was in full swing now, the warm sun blazed brightly and temporarily blinded me as I drove down the narrow lane. There was only one main road running through the small village of Whitehaven, both sides fully lined with yellow daffodils. The star shaped heads bobbed gently in the breeze, snowdrops and crocuses filled in the extra gaps, birds tweeted in the trees and a fat bumblebee buzzed past lazily. Cherry blossom petals swirled down and formed a mass on the edge of the pavement, the sweet smell perfumed the air with hopes of warm weather soon returning. The Fox and Rabbit was at the heart of the village, completely full to the brim, despite the fact it was only early afternoon. Not a single picnic bench was free outside, and a couple of people took to leaning against the brickwork of the pub. Casually I entered through the side of the pub labelled, inn. A round fellow with a magnificent greying curled moustache approached me,

"Nice to meet you, I'm Nick."

"Tom Jones," I courteously replied, holding out my hand.

"You want a room I take it?"

"I've already got a room sorted."

Nick hummed for a moment as he checked his computer, "So you are. Tom Jones. Oh…oh I see. Police, eh?"

"That's right. Detective Inspector Tom Jones. I've been sent over to investigate the latest case."

"The one involving Dan? I thought the case was closed, last I heard he was about to be given life imprisonment."

I bowed my head, "His trial has only started today. My superintendent however isn't satisfied with the outcome of the recent investigation, he wants me to look into it."

The publican grunted and handed him the keys, "Suit yourself, it's an open and shut case in my eyes. But go ahead, feel free to upset everyone and don't act surprised when no-one thanks you either!"

I took the keys and glanced at the number before heading up the stairs; room number three was a tiny little cubbyhole with only a single bed, cupboard and washstand. The door hit the corner of the cupboard, making it a tight squeeze to push my large suitcase in as well as myself. After what seemed a long time unpacking my few things, I headed back out into the corridor and found a welcoming sign on a door labelled bathroom. Just another small cubby hole with the tiniest bath I had ever seen in my life, no shower and a rather dirty limescale stained toilet. I wondered to myself, how am I going to survive this place? It was approaching dinner time, I made my way down the stairs and aimed for the bar. As I neared the locals, they immediately stopped their jollity and clammed up and stared. Politely I bobbed my head,

"Evening."

Unsurprisingly no-one answered, picking up their drinks with serious expressions, they left at the rear into the pub garden. Quickly I ordered some pub grub and a cider, then hurriedly aimed for a cosy little nook away from the hubbub. An elderly scruffy looking man in country attire and thick muddy walking boots with the soles peeling off, continued to stare unblinkingly. Awkwardly I turned to stare out of the window and pretended not to notice, the stranger however wasn't deterred, jumping off his bar stool he ambled over.

"Copper? Yeah, I thought so."

Not wanting to appear rude I turned to face him and politely grinned, "D.I. Tom Jones."

"Chris Horridge. I take it you're here about them murders. Aren't ya? Yeah, I thought so. You can see for yourself, the blood is still there in the wood. There was lots of blood I'm told…lots." The man wheezed into a dirty tissue and cleared his throat a few times, "Ai, there was bad blood spilt here that night…very bad indeed."

"Did you see what happened?"

"Nope. Nadda. I was at home, weren't I? It took two shots to bring them down, one for each of them. Of course, Nick replaced the glass, can't have this wind blowing through the brokenness can we now? You should be speaking to Jake about this. He's done very well for himself…very well indeed. I need a top up…you?"

My glass was nearly on the verge of emptiness, but before I could respond my sausages and mash arrived accompanied with an onion flavoured gravy. The lady left and resumed her post behind the bar, her kindly face and warm heartedness uplifted the atmosphere.

"That'd be Jackie. Nick's missus," Chris continued, settling down next to me and helped himself to a sausage, "She's the best thing that ever happened to this place. She and Nick would know a thing or two about that day, they were here when it all happened. Who else? Izzy Crow, lives around the corner, Dan were her boyfriend. Oh, look sharp. That's Simon coming in now, and he don't like coppers."

I looked up and immediately recognised the young man from earlier, he scowled in my direction and headed out, a cold blast of air blew through as he slammed the door shut.

"He don't like coppers," Chris repeated, raising his empty glass at Jackie and gave her a nod, "He were Ben's best friend. He convinced himself that Jake is behind it, but it was Dan who had the gun…not Jake."

"Dan was actually found with the murder weapon?" I gasped in shock.

"What I said weren't it? Here…you should talk with Mr Erroneous. He's the bobby here and he's more of an idiot than I am. Good luck D.I. Jones, you're going to need it."

Chris stood up and resumed his post at the bar, I could see him whispering to some people, who turned to gaze at me like I was a monkey in a zoo. My head was overwhelmed with so much information and yet I still had no idea what had actually happened that evening, a trip to see the local plod didn't sound like a bad idea.

*

The following morning after a quick trip to the bathroom, I wasn't surprised in the least on my return to find someone had pinned a note on my door saying, GO HOME COPPER. I tore the sheet of paper from the door and scrunched it up into a ball, I was more determined than ever now to stay put. After a grisly breakfast of hard bacon and raw fried eggs, I prepared myself for the day and ventured out for a decent coffee in town. There was only one café in the village, The Little Maple. Fortunately, it had only just opened a few minutes earlier and I was spoilt for choice where to sit. I decided to opt for the small table with two chairs by the bay window and watch the world go by and observe. A young brunette in her early thirties was quick to notice my arrival and floated over, she pulled out her notebook and pen,

"What can I get you sir?"

Quickly I scanned through the menu, "Cappuccino and a bacon and fried egg roll please."

She headed over to the counter and crashed around with the coffee machine, "Are you the policeman staying over at the pub?"

"Yes. D.I. Tom Jones."

"Not to sound rude Mr Jones, but you're not wanted in these parts. You've reached a dead end here…you should go home."

"Only when I'm satisfied with the case."

"Why aren't you satisfied?"

"Too many loose ends."

"Such as?"

I leaned back and thought quietly for a moment, "Let's just say for now that a lot of vital information is missing and it all seems too quickly solved, this investigation. There's not enough evidence or proof yet, that's the problem."

The girl headed over with my breakfast and hot drink, carelessly plonking them down and spilt hot coffee in the saucer, she then silently mumbled in my ear, "Prove it then. Prove to me that my Dan didn't commit the murders."

My body must have gone rigid at that point for all I could do was stare, "Are you Izzy Crow? I heard that you were Dan's girlfriend."

"I was," Izzy replied sadly and scribbled down something on her notepad, tore the sheet and handed it to me. "I've got customers. If you want to speak to me, here's my address."

I took the paper and neatly folded it into a smaller rectangle and pushed it into my breast pocket, watched Izzy leave to the other side of the café, then began on my delicious meal. Scraping up the yolk with the last of the bread, I paid up and sauntered outside, the sunrays warmed my back as I continued onwards to the other end of town. I was very impressed to see a gym squashed in the middle of the various charity shops, however it wasn't busy inside apart from one person breaking a sweat on the treadmill. The local businesses caught my attention and soon I was browsing inside each shop to see what wares they were selling and bought a few useless mementos. Upon my arrival at the police station, I was disappointed to find the constable in charge of the case was on the beat and wouldn't be back till lunchtime. Another young police officer however offered up his services and invited me to join him at his desk,

"Constable James Wright is out, can I help? I'm Constable Leon Nailer."

I shook his hand and sat down on a wooden chair which wobbled under my weight, "D.I. Tom Jones. I'm investigating the murders which happened back in December, I'm worried that the case is far from over."

"You mean Ben and Joe being snuffed like a candle? Can't help you there, I was at home that night. And there's nothing to worry about inspector, Wright solved the case and arrested the guy. Why are you looking into it? I don't understand."

"Is there a report I can read?"

Constable Nailer sighed and groaned, then hauled himself up and pulled out some drawers from the filing cabinet, he chuckled to himself, "Sorry. It's here somewhere…not this drawer anyhow…maybe here…?"

I clicked my tongue impatiently and checked my watch, Nailer eventually swung round with a thin folder and tossed it towards me, "Here. Should be all there."

"Is that it!?" I exclaimed, picking up a sheet of paper.

"Looks like it. I didn't 'Wright' it up…did I?" Constable Nailer guffawed loudly and smacked the table, "See what I did there?"

I wasn't amused in the slightest and set my eyes on the one piece of paper and began to read:

Daniel Cooper 38 years old, lives in Whitehaven at the Old Schoolhouse.

Today (Saturday 10th December 2022) at 3.30pm I was called to The Fox and Rabbit, there had been a murder you see. I went there and there was Ben Byrd and Joseph Rogers both had been shot through the heart, there was blood everywhere. Nick told me what happened, the lights went out, two shots were heard, and the window was broken. Everybody was panicking and screaming according to Nick. I took statements from the witnesses, a fat woman with *brown or red hair came forward and she said that Dan isn't Dan at all. According to her, he's a man called Dylan Worthy and he had murdered before. I arrested him and searched his pockets, and he still had the gun on him. I put him in the car and took him to the police station, the time now is 4.10pm.*

"Is that it!?" I found myself repeating, "Who wrote this? A child?"

"That would be me," a voice called through. I looked up and saw a very young police officer removing his helmet and placing it neatly on the table. He glared at me and asked, "Who are you?"

I gruffly introduced myself and refused to shake his hand, "This is a disgrace! Call yourself a policeman!? Where's the forensic reports? Any pictures of the crime scene? And where's the rest of the witness statements?"

"Don't be too hard on Wright. He's still learning, and this is his first murder." Constable Nailer spoke up, offering me a cup of watery tea with no milk. "Look inspector, the thing is…we're village coppers. We deal with petty theft, small disputes amongst friends, minor car crime, lost pets…do you get the picture? A major crime like this is completely out of our league. Wright caught the guy, now let's leave it at that, shall we?"

"Who's your superior? Tell them I want a word."

"Sunning herself I should imagine. Somewhere in the Canaries, I forget where."

"For crying out loud!" I rudely exclaimed, pushing the tea to one side and accidently knocked the liquid onto the floor.

Constable Wright stepped forward and grabbed a mop from the corner, "That wasn't called for! I'm sorry I messed up Inspector Jones, but we caught the guy. So, what's the problem?"

"Did you *really* catch the killer? How certain are you?"

Wright's face flushed and his cheeks glowed red, "I...the thing is. The thing is...I'm not one-hundred percent, I did have my doubts at the time. So...maybe sixty?"

"Sixty isn't good enough! Right, in your statement you mentioned the gun. Where is the gun now?"

"That'd be locked up in the vault," Nailer intervened, passing me a small key. Wright snatched the key off him before I had a chance and led me into the back office and down a flight of steep stairs. A piece of string dangled from the ceiling, I pulled it, and the light instantly came on to reveal a dark and murky cellar, full of fine cobwebs and lush moss pushing its way through the windowsill. Constable Wright fiddled with a number padlock attached to a large filing cabinet, then inserted the key into a minute keyhole.

"Here we are inspector."

I didn't waste a second in pulling on plastic gloves and carefully picked up the gun, realising what I was holding my temper got the better of me, "YOU ARE AN IDIOT, CONSTABLE JAMES WRIGHT!"

Constable Wright stared at me dumbfounded and bewildered, "That's the gun I found on Daniel Cooper inspector, it's not loaded or anything. I checked."

"THIS IS A REPLICA GUN! IT WOULDN'T BE LOADED WOULD IT!? YOU CAN'T EVEN FIRE THIS CERTAIN TYPE OF REPLICA!"

"But I've got the bullets that forensics gave me. Look."

I took the bullets and gave them a hard stare, "This looks like they belong to a rifle. How could you even think for a moment they'd belong to the other gun?"

"Well…I did think it was a bit odd." Wright admitted, putting everything back in the cupboard.

"A bit odd? A BIT ODD!?"

"Whoa!" cried a voice from the top of the stairs, "What's with all the shouting?"

Wright quickly explained the situation to Constable Nailer, who just stood there stupidly grinning and sarcastically responded, "Oops!"

"You said forensics gave you the bullets? Right?" I asked of Wright who was locking the cabinet door, "Did they give you a report?"

"They did," Nailer answered, clambering down two steps, "It's on my desk somewhere."

"FIND IT!" I demanded and turned back to Constable Wright, "We need to find the right gun and talk to as many people as possible. We need suspects and witnesses!"

"Sure, just tell me what to do and I'm your man."

Constable Nailer laughed quietly, "Whatever. Chasing ghosts isn't my style."

"What's it to you Nails? You were the one who said we should sweep this whole investigation under the carpet, I wanted to inform our sergeant first thing. You landed us both in hot water!" Constable Wright snapped and then resolutely addressed me, "Let's go."

Inwardly I grinned and followed the determined policeman up the steps and out the door, Constable James Wright wasn't so pathetic after all. Sure, he was bumbling and dim-witted, but he was definitely willing to prove his worth and clean up the mess he had created. There was a good chance now that perhaps Dan wasn't the actual killer, however, there were still too many coincidences in play to rule him out just yet.

Chapter 11

Clinging tightly to the handle of the passenger door and wishing that I didn't have two large breakfasts, the little Peugeot eventually parked up with one last almighty bump into a small courtyard. Constable Wright donned on some wellies from the boot of his car and sauntered towards the main barn, I hung back and waited for the queasy feeling in my stomach to subside. I noticed that I was being curiously watched by a very young man, his feeble arms shook as he lifted a haybale onto his shoulder and dropped it sideways onto a neat pile. An elderly well-weathered man, hobbling with a cane, headed in my direction,

"Eyeing the new boy, are we?"

Unsure what to say I nodded, "He looks like he could do we some help."

Ollie shook his head, "He'll be fine. Just needs to muster up some strength that's all. He can't do any damage sorting out the haybales. You look out of place here, what is it you want?"

"D.I. Jones. I'm looking into the recent murders…"

"Thought that was done and dusted," the farmer interrupted and patted my back, "Best come in then, you look like you need some tea to get rid of that peaky look. Bumpy ride, was it? I should have that road fixed really, potholes are a menace. I assume Wright is about? That's his car, isn't it?"

Oliver didn't wait for a reply and was already heading into the farmhouse, I couldn't see Constable Wright anywhere, so I followed inside after the farmer. I sat down by the little wooden table in the kitchen, two border collies bounded in and sniffed my trousers and one began to tug at my shoelaces. Suddenly the door burst open and a middle aged man with protruding biceps under his short sleeve shirt, gazed in my direction before shouting at the dogs,

"Go on Jessie and Larch! Outside both of you!"

The dogs whined and their tails hung down between their legs, obediently they trotted out of the farmhouse, very much subdued as if they'd just been scolded. The man sat down opposite me and accepted the tea that Ollie passed him, he was very much at home in the little kitchen as he removed his steel capped boots. The twiggy little boy I noticed earlier had managed to sneak in and was sitting quietly in the corner munching a chocolate digestive. Just as I thought things couldn't get any stranger, the door burst open one more time and Constable Wright ambled through, his clean wellies were now covered in mud.

"Where were you?" Wright panted, fixing his gaze on the muscly male whilst removing his thick coat, "I've been up and down the fields looking for you!"

Flexing his strong arms, the man smirked at him and scratched his bristly chin, "Mr Erroneous. What can I help you with now? I thought you were going to leave me alone?"

"I was," the policeman replied and sat in the seat between me and the other man, "But the D.I. here wants to speak to you…you know…about Ben and Joe."

"D.I. Tom Jones," I responded on cue and took a biscuit Ollie was offering me.

"Jake," The man replied with a nod of his head. Jake slowly turned to see if the young lad was listening to our conversation, but fortunately he was too engrossed in his phone. Jake called to him, "Oi Stevens! Chickens need feeding."

"Yes Mr Byrd! Straight away sir!" Stevens responded and legged it out the door.

Jake chuckled and slurped his hot tea, "That boy has a lot to learn, that was his third break today. What did you want to ask me?"

"Everything." I replied solemnly, placing my cup down, "I need to know about everything, everyone and every event that took place that fateful day."

The farmhand whistled slowly and rubbed his greying hair, "Right…where shall I begin?"

"You can start of by saying that Ben was your brother." Constable Wright enthused, pulling his notebook out, "And you can also tell Jones here that Dan was your best friend."

"Really?" I exclaimed loudly with surprise, "Go on."

Jake coughed a few times and calmly sipped his tea, "Ok, so Ben was my brother. He was a complete pain in the arse and I'm happy that he's no longer around to ruin my life. Satisfied?"

"He wants to know what led up to the murders Jake," Wright put in slamming his pen down, "He doesn't need to hear how much you two hated each other."

"Actually, I do." I stated, eyeing Jake curiously, "A lot of murderers I know are the ones who hate enough to kill."

"Well put Inspector Jones." Constable James Wright applauded, "Go on then Jake. Tell him everything."

Jake snarled at the two of them, "It wasn't just me who hated Ben, Dan hated him too you know! Izzy didn't like him much either. Anyway, the gun was fired from outside the pub not inside. Me and Dan were both in the toilets at the time of the shooting, which means it wasn't us."

"I'm not blaming you or anyone, I just want a rundown of what happened that day and what led up to it." I carefully explained in an attempt to calm Jake down.

"It was the Santa run that day…"

"Santa run?"

"Everyone dressed up as Santa or something Christmassy for a charity run in memory of George Lawson, Nick and Jackie's son, he died in the lake thirteen years ago. We were all there that day, me, Dan, Izzy, Izzy made a new friend, but I don't know her name. Ben, Ben's friend Simon and then Joe."

"Is that the Joe who's also been killed?"

"Yes. Joseph Rogers. Isabelle's latest boyfriend. Dan hated him passionately for dating Izzy, personally I found him alright, he offered me a job when I was at my lowest." Jake explained, finishing off a fourth biscuit.

I hummed thoughtfully to myself, "So Dan had good reason to see Ben *and* Joe dead, did he? And how do you mean Joe offered you a job, I thought you worked here?"

Ollie coughed awkwardly, "Ah, well you see…I fired him. Jake allegedly sold my sheep, Jake explained to me that it was Ben who sold the sheep, not him. Ben was working for me at the time you see. Naturally I gave Jake his job back, best farmhand I've ever had, it was wrong of me to fire him in the first place, and I've regretted it ever since."

"Ok," I responded understanding the situation, "Go on then Jake. What happened that day?"

"I'm not going to remember everything inspector, it was three months ago." Jake continued and stared at the ceiling in thought, "Let's see, since you're going to find out one way or another you might as well know, me and Ben came to blows just before the race. He was going to tell everyone that I stole the sheep if I lost the race, but if I *won* the race then he would admit it was him. Naturally that dope cheated and won the race, cut through the bottom field, didn't he? Once everyone arrived at the finish line we went in for drinks, I believe Joe said something cutting to Dan, Dan was in a right foul mood after him and Joe had a quiet talk on the side. Joe had been belittling Dan all day."

"Then what happened?"

"Drinks and food, the Lawson's laid a banquet out for the village. Then I went to the loo, Dan followed. Next thing, we're hearing two loud bangs from a gun. We charged back in, found the girls terrified under a table so we went over to them. Next thing the girl with Isabelle is screaming her head off and pointing to two dead bodies by the bar. Nick rushed in and took over the situation. Mr Erroneous then turned up and arrested Dan for murder because a woman told him to, and according to the obese cow, Dan is called Dylan, and he has murdered before."

Constable James Wright scoffed loudly, "You know that's rubbish! She's got Dan mixed up with someone else whose name is Dylan. And I found a gun in

Dan's pocket, that's the real reason why I arrested him, not because some woman told me to!"

"Whatever Mr Erroneous. You always do what you're told and never use your own initiative." Jake smirked, pushing himself out of the chair. "We done? I have work to get on with. Busy month March."

I nodded and also stood up, "One more thing. Do you think Dan is the killer?"

Jake firmly shook his head, "No. Dan is too soft, he's never even been in a scrap. And as I said, we were in the gents when it all kicked off. Neither of us went outside."

"Who do you think the killer is?"

"How would I know? Obviously, it was a random shooting or someone else wanting to kill my stupid brother. Ben has plenty of enemies, shouldn't take you too long to find someone else who hates his guts."

"Do you believe Ben to be the initial target and not Joe?"

Jake shrugged his broad shoulders, "Who knows inspector. If you want me again, come in the evening, I'm at Primrose Cottage. I'll be seeing you, Mr Erroneous."

We watched him stride out the farmhouse with speed, the dogs who had been waiting impatiently outside, now barked and danced around his ankles with delight. Oliver mumbled something about a lame lamb, and he too headed outside, leaving us behind in a suddenly silent kitchen. The sun was gradually descending and disappearing over the horizon as we squelched through the muddy yard and zigzagged past the chickens pecking at our toes. Having no more suggestions or ideas what to do next, we made our way back to The Fox and Rabbit for a friendlier meal to make up for earlier. Once again, the pub was full to the brim with drinkers, most of whom were propping up the bar. It wasn't a surprise when the villagers starting to jeer the moment they noticed our presence, Nick came across to us and sat down at the next table,

"Ignore them. Heard you'd been speaking to Jake."

"Too right we have," Constable James Wright squeakily answered, struggling with the tight clip under his chin and finally removed his helmet, "He didn't have much to say though, just gave us a rundown on what happened that day."

Nick chortled, "We all know what happened. Two men were shot down, right at the bar."

"Were they sitting or standing at the bar?" I enquired, tucking into my pie and mash.

"Standing I believe."

"And which pane of glass did you replace? Chris mentioned it last night."

Nick grumbled and pointed out a piece of glass which looked cleaner than the others, "That one."

"That's very low down." I exclaimed, standing up to observe the window, "Barely comes up to my waist!"

"What have you noticed inspector?" Wright asked enthusiastically, pulling out his notepad, "Is it a clue?"

"Not really," I replied, staring outside at the front pub garden, "There's some hedges out there. I reckon whoever it was, was hiding behind the hedge most likely with bended knees."

"Right. Right." said Constable Wright, scribbling it all down in his little book, "Sorry inspector, I don't follow."

"It means, whoever fired the gun must firstly have great aim and secondly be very fit to be able to shoot in such an awkward and uncomfortable position. Or of course it could have been a very tiny man or woman."

"Jake is very fit and athletic. But then so is Daniel, did you know he's a gardener? Then there's Simon, he's the local builder."

"Isabelle Crow? She's not athletic but she is very small."

The young constable gave a very loud snort, alarming the couple opposite us, he exclaimed, "Izzy! You must be joking! Wasn't she under the table when the gun went off?"

"Jake says he *found* her under the table. He didn't know when or how long she was there for, remember, he only turned up after he heard the commotion."

"Or so he says."

I sighed very loudly with annoyance and followed Nick up to the bar to replenish my empty pint glass, it was all 'he says or 'she says', there was no actual witnesses yet, only word of mouth. Was anything anyone said the absolute truth? Or was everyone deliberately lying to my face? I looked down at my feet and immediately noticed the stains in the flooring, the only one piece of concrete evidence being the mark left behind from the murders. At least Chris wasn't lying about that. So, Ben and Joe must have been standing on this very spot when they were shot, the only spot in the pub to be in full view of the window. Was it a coincidence? Now, who was with them at the bar? Jake, Daniel, Simon and Izzy and one other girl. It was vital that I find the other girl to give Isabelle an alibi for the time of the murders. Jake and Dan were going toilet, they could easily have given each other an alibi. And Simon, where was he at the time of the murders? Where was he now?"

"Hey Nick," I called, leaning across the counter, "Is Simon out the back?"

Nick passed me an overflowing pint of lager, "Should be. I reckon he's avoiding you, he don't like…"

"He don't like coppers. I heard. Why doesn't he like coppers? Is there something that happened to him to make him hate coppers so much?"

The publican put down the pint glass he was filling and quietly mumbled, "Simon used to run a building company a few years ago with Ben. There was something dodgy going on there, you can bet on it. Dodgy material being used, income tax being avoided, shifty foreign workers, you name it. Police rushed in on the place and immediately shut it down. Now Simon is working for a legit building firm on a lower pay and he's not happy about it, Ben on the other hand ran back to his mother."

"I see. One more thing Nick. Where was Simon when the murders kicked off?"

"Hmm. You know what, I have no idea. It never occurred to me that Simon was absent at the time we discovered Ben and Joe."

"But he was there that day?"

"Of course he was, he was at the bar with Joe and Ben having a drink when the lights went out. Not sure what happened to him after that, he must have left the building."

I nodded, picked up my drink and thanked Nick, then headed outside into the garden in search for Simon

Harper. A small group of surly looking men spotted me and pushed their heavy bodies up from the picnic bench and folded their thick arms. I didn't feel comfortable in the least as the men slowly strode towards me in an attempt to intimidate me further. Simon however ignored the situation at hand and carried on drinking at the little table, he also turned a deaf ear to me calling out to him. Nick thankfully was right behind me collecting empty glasses.

"OI! Simon! Jonesy here wants a word!" Nick shouted, throwing a coaster at the man's head then turned to face the larger blokes, "And you can back off! Unless you want barring from the pub!"

The men growled then subsided, having no desire to be barred from their favourite local; a man took a thundering sudden step towards me and succeeded in startling me. Simon chuckled with satisfaction and mumbled what sounded like 'wimp' under his breath. Choosing to ignore that rude comment, I sat directly opposite him and plonked my full glass down on the table and bobbed my head,

"Simon."

"Copper." Simon replied, wiping the froth from his upper lip, "What do you want? You've been watching me the past few days."

"Not intentionally, but you are a suspect in the case. I have a few questions."

"Shoot."

"Where were you on Saturday 10th December?"

"How should I know?" Simon answered, swinging his legs round from under the picnic bench and stood up to leave.

"It was the day of the Santa run. I only want to know where you were and where you disappeared to when the lights turned off. Obviously, you went somewhere, otherwise you wouldn't be here right now talking to me, you would be dead." I loudly explained to him in an effort to stall him from going back into the pub.

Simon halted and sighed with annoyance, then hesitated for a moment and swung back round to face me with a wicked grin, "Stealing."

My face must have shown confusion and surprise, as Simon burst out in uncontrollable laughter.

I snapped irritably, "What do you mean stealing!?"

"Just that. The lights went out and I took the opportunity. Not the first time the lights have gone out either."

"You've stolen before?"

"Oh yeah. Loads of times." Simon grinned smugly, opening the back door to The Fox and Rabbit, "Unfortunately for you though, there won't be CCTV. Nick doesn't have high-tech night-vision cameras…and unless someone complains about their missing items, I'm rather off the hook. Aren't I? Be seeing you copper."

For the first time in ages, I was speechless and stared stupidly at the door that was slowly closing, I couldn't believe that Simon so openly admitted to stealing. He must be lying about his whereabouts, why else would he tell such a shocking lie.

"Penny for your thoughts?" Nick chortled, patting me on the back.

"I need to look at your CCTV for the day of the murders." I sternly stated, following the publican back to the bar.

Nick chuckled nervously and carefully hung up his dirty tea-towel, "Ah. That might be a problem. You see…on the actual day of the murders, someone disconnected the cameras. I already explained that to Constable Wright."

"Who disconnected the cameras?"

"How should I know? I was a bit preoccupied with the race and lunch and everything else. I didn't even realise the cameras were out till I offered to show that bumbling policeman the footage, only to realise that there was no footage to show."

"Right. When was the last time you had a blackout?"

"Not since the murders. I had a blackout though a few days before the murders. Think it was Wednesday. Do you want to see the tape?"

"Please." I answered and followed through into the little office at the back of the pub, Nick plumped up a cushion and threw it down on a swivel chair, then carefully perched himself on top. After much hawing he eventually found the right day and time,

"Here we are," said Nick perking up and smiled. "9pm on Wednesday 7th December."

I sat down in the chair next to him and carefully watched the footage, to my amazement the gang were all there that night, Daniel, Jake, Ben, Simon, Joseph and Isabelle. Isabelle and Joseph soon left after what appeared to be a very hurried drink, Izzy hadn't even touched hers. Unfortunately, there was no sound on the tape, suddenly the screen blackened, and the night-vision flicked on.

"Hey!" I exclaimed with astonishment, "I thought you didn't have night-vision?"

The publican grunted, "Who told you that? I had new cameras installed a year ago now, we've been having problems with thievery you see."

Suddenly a fight broke out between three of the four men, it started off with a small scuffle which quickly escalated. I found myself wincing as Jake managed to get his younger brother in an uncomfortable headlock, Dan intervened and managed to loosen Jakes's grip, only to find himself being punched in the stomach by Ben.

"Bit like the movies," Nick quietly laughed as he watched himself appear on screen to separate the men. "Feels weird watching yourself on TV."

"What are they fighting over?" I asked Nick and then quietly murmured to myself, "And where is Simon?"

Nick shrugged his shoulders, "Those two are always arguing or fighting over something. You should talk to the mum. Whew, I bet she can tell you a story or two!"

I watched the film for a little longer, hoping that Simon would return back to the screen, unfortunately he didn't, he was nowhere to be seen. Nick turned off the computer screen and leaned back,

"Hope that was useful to you inspector."

"It was in a way. Do you know where Mrs Byrd lives?"

The publican guffawed loudly with amusement, "Mrs Byrd? No one has ever called her that before! She's called Rita, lives down Church Street. Aim for the Church and you'll find her, number four."

"Thank you." I responded, making my way out to the main door of the pub, it was late evening now, but hopefully Jake and Ben's mum should be home.

A voice suddenly sounded behind me, "Where we off to then?"

I cursed silently to myself, I had completely forgotten about my young assistant, "Constable Wright. I'm off to talk to Rita Byrd about her sons."

"*We're* off," Constable Wright annoyingly corrected and held the door open for me, "Car is round the side inspector. Good luck talking to Rita, that woman sure knows how to talk the hind leg off a donkey!"

"Why drive when we can walk constable? And don't worry, I enjoy the company of old people."

Chapter 12

Number four Church Street was a pretty picture, daffodils and muscari completely filled the front garden, with sweet pink hyacinths popping out of pots by the wooden bay windows. The house was directly opposite the Church; the only thing that came between the buildings were two stone walls and the little road. It was a peaceful road with no cars parked anywhere, a picturesque scene of what time would have looked like in the fifties. Wright opened the picket gate and ambled up to the front door and knocked loudly with the lion knocker. A timid, old, frail looking woman peered through the net curtains and recognising the police officer she waved to the front door. Constable Wright seemed to understand the signalling and opened the door for us then called out,

"Evening Rita. Sorry it's late. Inspector wants a word."

Mrs Byrd didn't seem to mind and welcomed us into the living room, "Come in then, keep the cold out. James, be a good boy and make us some tea."

Gently she took my hand and guided me towards a chair, I could feel the bones of her fingers protruding under her cold thin skin. She lowered herself down on a high armchair and sighed with fatigue.

"Tiring, isn't it? Getting old," she exclaimed, picking up a photo frame from the table.

Unsure how to reply to such a comment, I awkwardly shrugged my shoulders.

"Here," Rita continued and passed me the photo for me to look at, "My boys. I suppose that's what you're here for? James has already asked me questions, but I assume you have more to ask?"

Expecting to see a recent picture of the brothers, I was rather surprised to see it was a younger photo, Jake looked only about twelve. They were both in swim trunks and had goggles with snorkels on their heads, both of them were smiling and had their arms over each other's shoulders. Ben, even though he was younger than Jake, towered over his older brother and was definitely larger in size too. Jake was painfully scrawny with ribs showing and his swimming trunks had string around them to hold them up.

Rita took the picture back and lovingly cleaned the glass with a cloth, "That was our last holiday to the seaside. Just before my husband, the boys' father, died of a heart attack. He was only fifty-three."

"I'm sorry." I mumbled, sitting down in the armchair opposite.

"So am I. That's when life went downhill pretty fast, I had to get a job which meant less time with the boys, which led to the boys fighting more. Fortunately, when they grew up and left school, Jake got a decent job and a decent house with a wife and child. Ben however was always trouble, he managed to start up a building firm which went bust, lost all of his money and came home crying to me. Couldn't secure a job after that, he refuses to work for anyone, so I made him work for me, odd errands around the house and so on."

The sound of china trembling and clinking could be heard, as Constable Wright nervously carried the tray round the corner and placed it down with a clatter onto the coffee table, "Tea Rita? I've used your best china since it's a formal occasion."

"Is it?" Rita asked surprised and took the cup and saucer from Constable Wright, "I thought you were just asking routine questions?"

"We are." I answered, "I just want to talk to someone who really knew Ben and who might have an idea who killed him. Do you know who might?"

Rita sadly shook her head and wiped away a tear, "Ben was beautiful. Really beautiful. He's looked after me for the last twelve years, I wouldn't be living here without him. They want to put me in a home you see…Jake and Maisy. Ben always helped others, despite the fact that he had hardly any money of his own. He owes a lot of people money now, that might have caused him to be killed."

"Did you know he had a new job at the farm?"

"Oh yes, I forgot about that, James told me. Oliver was so kind to offer my Ben work and a home. Dead chuffed I was. But still…" said Rita and darkly added, "Whoever killed my son…I want them to suffer for what they did, put into a cell and have the key thrown away."

"And do you think you might know who killed him?" Constable Wright asked, plopping three sugar cubes into his tea.

Rita Byrd shook her head dismally, "No, I don't. Yes, I know you arrested Daniel for the murders, but Daniel is too soft. Do you remember James, when Ben and Simon tricked Jake into meeting them at The King's Head? Ben was apparently going to give Jake his motorbike back. Turned out they had plans for Jake and were going to throw him into the lake. Daniel didn't stop them or intervene, he ran back to The Fox and Rabbit and called you from there, do you remember?"

Constable firmly nodded his head and accidently spilt his tea over his hand, "That's right! Happened a few days before Ben died…Anyway, by the time I got there it was all over. Nick and some mates of his sorted the situation out, sent Ben and Simon packing."

"And the bike?" I enquired.

"Dunno. My guess is Ben sold it after stealing it. He's always in need of money and not bothered how low he has to stoop in order to get it either."

"That's a wicked thing to say about my son!" Rita angrily stated, pointing a stern finger at the policeman, "Ben is not a thief! It's that friend of his, Simon, who's a thief. Ask anyone in the village, every shop owner has their eye on *him*."

Constable Wright turned bright red and tried to hide his face in his collar, "Sorry Rita. I shouldn't have said that."

Rita glowered at him and replied, "No. Too right you shouldn't!"

I promptly jumped up and gently shook hands with Rita, "Well. Thank you for talking to us Rita. We best be going now."

The younger policeman couldn't get to the door quick enough and rapidly said, "Yes. Thank you, Rita."

It was cold outside despite being spring, the wind howled and whipped around us, and a large raindrop splattered on my coat. The streetlights weren't working properly and flickered constantly, nobody was out on this dark night. A ghostly barn owl screeched as it swooped silently down over our heads in the direction of the Church roof.

"Blummin' bird!" Constable Wright muttered to himself, "Nearly took my helmet off!"

"Are you always that polite when talking to elderly people?" I enquired, kicking a stone with the toe of my shoe. "Rita could've done without that snide remark about Ben."

"Well...I..."

"Maybe you should keep comments like that to yourself from now on and avoid unnecessary upset. I'll see you tomorrow officer. I want to talk to Izzy and hopefully she can tell us more about Daniel and possibly Joseph."

"Yes sir. Oh...one more thing. Is it true? That Dan really is this other man, Dylan. It's the talk of the village what that woman said, you know, when she said that Dan was really a murderer called Dylan."

I sighed tiredly, "Five years ago I arrested a man called Dylan on suspicion of murdering two people. The jury voted not guilty, but I think they're wrong. And it's been proven via fingerprints that Dylan Worthy changed his name to Daniel Cooper and moved to Whitehaven."

The young officer whistled, "So Daniel *is* a murderer called Dylan? But he's in prison now, so what are you actually investigating if the murderer is behind bars? I caught the guy, I've been right this whole time!"

The rain was coming down harder now and began to soak through my clothing, "I need to be sure this time, I need evidence, I need witnesses, I need motives. I don't want another shamble like last time."

"We need to talk to that woman who knew Dan was Dylan. I think she was staying at the B&B at Redstone Farm. Maybe we can find out where she is now."

I smiled at the younger policeman, "You know Constable Wright. That's the best suggestion you've had all day. Right, see you."

Constable Wright beamed proudly, "Thank you. Night sir."

*

"It's just around this corner now sir. It should be at the end of the crescent."

I rolled my eyes with annoyance as the car neared the other end of the road, I had no desire to keep going round and around in circles, I parked the car with a sudden dramatic stop. Number thirty-two was nowhere to be seen, "There's twenty-eight and the last house. Maybe we should ask someone."

"Hang on a moment sir," Wright continued, prodding his phone and squinting, "It's not coming up on google maps. How about we…? Sir?"

I had enough and was already out of the vehicle and knocking on doors, hoping for directions from one of the neighbours. A scrawny middle aged woman abruptly opened her door, wiping her bubbly hands on a tea-towel,

"What?"

"Sorry to trouble you. We're looking for thirty-two."

"One of the new houses, right? Top of the crescent. There's a small road to the right."

"Thank…"

The woman had already slammed the door shut in my face before I could even finish my sentence. Feeling more annoyed than ever, I reversed the car back up the road to find a small side road with four new looking houses. The house was right at the end with a small Mini parked on a driveway stained with orange paint and a broken glued-back-together gnome. A dark brown cat watched us intensely with bright green eyes, then jumped down to hide in the next door neighbour's garden.

"What happened here? Looks vandalised." I stated, jumping out of the car.

Wright joined my side as we headed up to the front door, "That'll be Dan's work. I cautioned him couple of months back for throwing paint on Joe's Mercedes, breaking Isabelle's gnome and waving a dangerous knife about."

"And we're supposed to believe he is too soft for murder?" I snorted and rang the doorbell. Izzy had been expecting us and promptly opened the door to let us in. We're followed through into the living room and plonked ourselves down on the large sofa and found our bodies sinking awkwardly into the soft fabric. Isabelle wandered off back into the kitchen to make the coffee whilst we observed the house furnishings and the many family photos on the wall. The room reeked of paint fumes, so I opened the window slightly to let the fresh air in; my arm brushed the window sill and white paint transferred onto my sleeve. Suddenly a cat leapt through and landed gracefully at my feet, it was the same cat from earlier, she purred affectionately and rubbed my leg. Isabelle who had calmly come into the room, quickly slammed the mugs of coffee down and ran to the window,

"You mustn't open it! Leonardo could get out and he's an indoor house cat."

I profusely apologised as Izzy slammed the window shut and sprayed the room with a sweet-pea air freshener. She left again to fetch something sweet to eat as Constable Wright exaggeratedly coughed and spluttered,

"Why do females use so much spray? I'm pretty sure Leonardo would be much happier with the window open than having to smell that awful air freshener!"

I elbowed him roughly in the ribs as Izzy returned with a plateful of biscuits, and four cats twisted around her ankles which jumped onto her lap the moment she sat down. She looked rather like a witch or a mad woman as she sat in the dark corner stroking her cats.

"So, which one is Leonardo?" Wright asked making polite conversation, then lifted his coffee off the table.

Isabelle pointed to the black cat on her lap, "Him. But you're not here to talk about my cats. Are you? You want to talk about Dan and how well I know him and whether I think he's a murderer? He is not. He is rather pathetic when it comes to standing up for himself. Dan had multiple chances to put Joe right, give him what for; instead, he vandalised Joe's car, cut off his water and electric and even spied on Joe when he cheated on me."

"Oh?" I exclaimed with surprise, "Joe, as in your latest boyfriend Joe? He cheated on you?"

"Dan turned up here the night before Joe and Ben…you know. Showed me pictures of Joe and Zoe having a cosy dinner at Joe's home, a romantic candlelit dinner I should add."

"Could they have just been friends?" Wright enquired meekly.

"They were kissing."

"Ah."

"They're not very good pictures, Dan was spotted and had to run back to his car. He told me he had taken better photos the night before when he spied on them at Ziggy's, but he got into an argument with Joe and Joe made sure he erased them," she explained then stood up and rummaged through a shelf piled high with letters and unopened post, eventually she pulled out an A5 envelope and tossed it at me, "Here. Says everything."

I pulled out the pictures from the packet and flicked through the photos, "Definitely cosy. Did Dan hope to win you back by telling you about Joe and Zoe?"

"Well…actually, I already knew about Zoe. Joe lied about a work meeting and when I confronted him, he admitted being in the Maldives with Zoe. Unfortunately, Dan was visiting me at the time and overheard the whole thing. I…erm…might have been the cause for the hostility between Joe and Dan. They spent a week feuding between each other, tit-for-tat, both fighting over me. Stupid really, because…"

"Because at the end of the day, it's Dan you'd rather be with," Constable Wright finished ramming another biscuit in his mouth and seeing my stern look immediately swallowed, before quick-wittedly asking, "Jake said you were with a girl the night Joe and Ben got killed. Who was she? Was it Zoe by any chance?"

Isabelle looked at her thumbs and twiddled them, "I didn't know she would be at the Santa run. But when I saw her, I took the opportunity to talk to her. Annoyingly, she is really nice, I like her a lot. I told her about Joe dating me and she didn't seem surprised at all, she actually laughed it off."

"Are you sure you didn't know about Zoe being at the Santa run? You don't sound sure." I inquisitively pressurised.

Izzy coughed sheepishly and hesitated, "Ok…ok…I had a feeling she'd be there, only a feeling mind. When Dan arrived at my house with the photos, he was sporting a nose bleed and a bruised lip. When I confronted him, he said he walked into a lamppost. As if! I said I'll give a Joe a hard time for what he did, and Dan just said, 'Leave it, I'll talk to them tomorrow'. Doesn't take much to put two and two together."

"We'll need to talk to her," I responded, scribbling down a mental note to find out where Zoe lived and worked, "Coming back to Dan, you said that he couldn't be the murderer. Do you have any idea who it could be?"

"No. Joe was a lying cheat and Ben was an irritating git. Anybody could have killed them."

"One last question, why did Dan send you photos of Zoe and Joe if you both already knew about their relationship?"

"When Joe admitted going to the Maldives with Zoe, he told me it was a mistake, and it was over between him and Zoe. I guess Dan wanted to prove that Joe was lying, and he was still carrying on with Zoe behind my back."

"Right, thank you Isabelle. We best be going."

Constable Wright courteously bobbed his head, grabbed his jacket and followed me out; gently pushing Leonardo away from the door with his toe as he shut it. He crashed into the passenger seat and pulled out a snickers from his pocket, ripped it open and took a large bite and sighed with satisfaction.

"I'm surprised you're hungry after all those biscuits," I grumpily remarked, finding my young constable's high metabolism rate very trying. Wright was one of those annoying people who could eat all day, binging on chocolate and biscuits and yet, not gain a single ounce on his thin body.

"What next sir?"

"Zoe next. You know, I still think there's a chance that Isabelle could have killed Joe," I pondered darkly, even though I had a gut feeling that it couldn't be. Placing the key in the ignition I started the car, "You can tell Isabelle hated him for cheating on her. So maybe Ben was an accident?"

"Or Zoe could have killed Joe, after Izzy told her that Joe was dating her at the same time. Making Ben an accident? Or could both girls be in it? Who said they saw the girls hiding under the table? Jake, was it?"

"Hmm. But then Jake was in the gents at the time, it was when he came back, he found them under the table. Who's to say they were there the whole time?"

"We need an eyewitness sir. And not one of the group but one of the locals."

I broadly grinned and patted Wright on the back, "You have the makings of a fine detective, with a little help, you can go far."

Constable Wright proudly beamed, "Think so? Thank you, sir."

The young man dug around the glove box and found a pack of spearmints, then triumphantly popped one into his mouth and silently chewed as he stared out of the window daydreaming. Detective Constable James Wright, England's most famous and celebrated detective of all time, and there would be a statue unveiling of him right in the heart of Whitehaven on the green.

Chapter 13

Slapton High School was positioned on the outskirts of Slapton, several large unattractive blocks of grey, stuck together haphazardly with a field plonked at the back. A tall spiked green fence surrounded the building keeping the children in and the public out, there was no entry safe for a small side entrance with an intercom. A trio of teenagers skiving off lessons sat on a bench-back, watching us suspiciously as they swung back Coca-Cola and listened to music on their phones. The gate buzzed open just as the bell rang for lunch, doors burst open and children spilled out in all directions, immediately we were swallowed up into the mass and found ourselves being herded towards the main hall. Spotting an empty classroom, I quickly jumped inside and waited for the stampede to pass, a young teacher shouted at the children to walk not run. Over by reception, a tall, weedy looking gentleman with a bobbled green cardigan hanging off stooped shoulders, peered curiously at me over the brim of his thin glasses,

"Can I help you sir?"

Realising I had been spotted I made my way over, "D.I. Jones."

"Deputy Headteacher Roy Tanner." Mr Tanner responded slowly and importantly, he gracefully removed his glasses, "I suppose I'm in charge now since our headteacher Joseph Rogers is dead. Strictly speaking, I've always been in charge, even when that little oik stole my headteacher job and made me inferior."

"Why was that?"

"I'm too old. Apparently, I run this school like they did in Victorian times. Not true strictly speaking, but the other teachers felt the same as Mr Rogers. There's nothing wrong with a bit of discipline, I always say. These children are unruly and need taking down a peg. However, that's not how schools are run nowadays, sadly. Mr Rogers doesn't believe in strict disciplinary action when a child has been misbehaving."

"I take it you don't like Mr Rogers?"

"No. I do not. Now Detective Inspector Jones. What brings you to my school?" Mr Tanner enquired and offered me a seat in the waiting area.

"I was hoping to speak to Zoe Turner?"

"Miss Turner, please, inspector. Children around here are extremely childish and it's best they don't start using teachers' Christian names around here. Miss Turner should be on a lunch break in the sixth form common room. I'll take you there now."

Expecting Mr Tanner to be an ageing tortoise, I was surprised at how agile he was as he sped off down the corridor with enormous strides. Grabbing my coat, (which had irritatingly got stuck in the chair and held me up for a moment), I quickened my pace and ran after him as he disappeared down another corridor. To my annoyance as I turned the corner, Mr Tanner the tortoise was nowhere to be seen. A door opening above my head alerted me to his presence as he quietly walked through; jumping up the stairs two at a time I made it to the sixth form common room.

"Miss Turner is though here," said Mr Tanner calmly and waved an arm towards a young teacher in the corner. "Now, excuse me. I'll be in my office having my lunch."

Zoe Turner was chuckling as she called me over to join her, "He's quick, isn't he? Mr Tanner."

I was thoroughly out of breath as I collapsed in the chair next to her, then introduced myself and replied, "For an old man, he completely caught me off guard. How old is he!?"

"Eighty-seven apparently. Here, let me fix you a drink. I've got a smoothie in the fridge?"

The door to the common room opened again, a cross looking teacher firmly guided a sheepish looking pupil across the room and through a door at the end labelled 'detention'.

Zoe passed me my drink and explained, "Tommy Brown. Spends most of the day in detention. He's not a bad kid but he is extremely disruptive and mischievous, the class clown."

"Shame," I responded, crossing my legs over and leaned back in my chair, "Miss Turner, I'm hoping you can answer some of my questions? Back in December when Joseph was killed, I want to know how well you knew him and who he was."

"Joe?" Zoe answered and blushed like a schoolgirl then sighed, "He was wonderful…decent, kind, generous. Then all that changed."

"Because he was killed?"

"Oh no. This was before he was killed. A little tart stole him from me, probably to do with the fact she wears tiny mini-skirts! Joe told me it was over between them. But then the tart's boyfriend showed up, first at Ziggy's pizzeria then in Joe's garden the next day, he was taking photos of us. I brushed it off, until I saw her again at the Santa run, we got talking and I only realised then that the boyfriend was trying to prove that me and Joe were a couple. Isabelle had no idea that Joe had been dating me for three years and it was *me* that he cheated on, her face was a picture! Isabelle was hoping that we could be friends after all this…yeah right."

"I take it you don't like Isabelle then? What about Isabelle's boyfriend, Dan?"

"I don't like either of them, I only got talking to them properly after the race, it was awful. Dan is too full of himself, and Isabelle is an obnoxious little twerp. It was no surprise when the bobby arrested Dan for the murders, I had a hunch it was him because he left the pub just before it happened. Also, he's been threatening Joe, loads of times apparently."

"Who said that? Joe?"

"Joe told me that Dan vandalised his car with paint, and when Joe confronted him, Dan pulled out a large knife and threatened to kill him. And then Dan cut of his electric and water, spied on us. Joe woke up to a threatening letter the day he was killed, it was posted through his door and written in red ink which looked like blood."

My ears pricked up at this piece of new information, I curiously asked, "Do you know where Joe put the letter?"

"I think he filed it away or burnt it most likely," Zoe replied, tidying away her lunch box.

"When you find it, let me know. It could be important. Did Joe and Dan ever come to blows?"

Zoe firmly shook her head, "No. Not in front of me anyway. Dan was more verbally threatening when I was around, not physically. You see, on the outside he seems charming, kind, shy, but there's a monster on the inside ready to pounce when no-one is looking. I know he killed Joe, and I can understand why. We had a girl here, Miss Castle. She rubbed Joe up the wrong way, got on his nerves, had better ideas when it came to teaching and so on; next thing we heard, she had been fired. Dan rubbed Joe up the wrong way too and Joe must have said something cutting to upset Dan enough to murder, I saw Joe and Dan talking together at the Santa run and it wasn't a friendly chat."

I reflected on the first time I met Daniel or Dylan as he was known then, but the only thing I could see in my mind was a monster, he never appeared kind or charming. I asked, "Do you know what Joe said?"

"Sorry no," Zoe replied just as the bell rang again, "Lunch is over. Back to the art room for me. Do you have my address? Next time, visit me at home. The walls here have ears, the whole school probably knows why you're here by now. Bye inspector."

The rest of the staff were also quick to leave, and I found myself on my own within a matter of minutes, I collected my coat and quietly left. Only a few female students lingered in the corridors and watched me intensely, then sniggered behind their hands as they whispered and giggled to each other. Mr Tanner politely escorted me off the premises and watched me drive off down the road before retreating back inside the school.

It was a slow drive back to Whitehaven, traffic lights and roadworks stalled me, only a few cars were allowed to pass through at a time. Fortunately, I had my mints to occupy me, I chewed silently and let my mind wander. Jake hated his brother but not Joe, Joe actually helped him at his hour of need. Dan hated Joe passionately, but did he hate Ben enough to kill him too? Isabelle blatantly loved Dan and hated Joe, would she kill for love? And Zoe…would you kill someone because they cheated? Not likely. The car behind me hooted like mad and I woke up from my daze and dragged my car two spaces forward. Then there was Simon, he had no alibi, but he had no motive either, Ben was his best friend. Nah, best leave Simon alone, he doesn't like the police, best not to aggravate him more than necessary! For now, Daniel was looking up to be my prime suspect, he had motive and no alibi. He had killed before but got away with it, it was all down to me to make sure he won't get away with it this time. Finally, the light turned green and the car in front slowly chugged along, my hand hovered over the horn and I just managed to squeeze through as the light changed back to red. I groaned with annoyance as the car refused to speed up and cruised along the slightly bendy country lanes at thirty miles, the driver behind me soon caught up and hooted his horn erratically once more.

*

It was nearly two in the afternoon when I pulled up at Whitehaven police station, Constable Wright saw me from the window and came running out,

"Where have you been sir!? There's been a development and I couldn't get hold of you!"

"What kind of development?" I demanded, following him inside and slammed the door shut, "Has someone finally confessed? Has Dan?"

"Nails is interviewing the suspect now."

A loud metallic clang rang out and the sounds of keys jangled as a lock was clicked into place. Constable Nailer whistled with jollity, his smug face revealed itself as he came round the corner and crashed into his office chair,

"He confessed."

"What!? Who!?" I loudly exclaimed with surprise, thumping my hand down on the desk, demanding to know exactly who we were talking about.

"Nick Lawson."

"Nick!? The publican from The Fox and Rabbit? Did he confess to both murders?"

"Murders?" Nailer asked confused and raised his legs up on the desk. "I was talking about the gun."

"Gun?"

Constable Wright passed me his habitual weak tea, "Nails found the rifle. Nick had it locked in his cellar, we got a tip off from one of the staff there. She heard we'd been looking for a rifle and when Nick lied about his rifle, she got suspicious and called the station."

"Just that." Constable Leon Nailer responded, "Nick said he found it outside. He was scared that a child might use it, so he put it in the cellar. But now he's confessed that the gun is actually his."

"Nick is part of some gun club."

"Yes, thank you Wright. Anyway, I'll talk to him later and get him to confess to the murders too."

"Are you telling me you found the actual gun? The right gun this time?" I asked, wringing my wrists in anticipation.

Constable Nailer scoffed loudly and unwrapped his egg and cress sandwich, "Course. Checked with ballistics and it's legit. Forensics checked for fingerprints and the only ones found were Nick's.

Placing my tea on a dusty shelf I asked, "Can I talk to him."

Nailer noisily slurped his tea, "Can't say no to my superior, can I."

Wright opened the door to the prison cells, then tossed me the keys, "Number three, on the left."

Not wasting a second, I headed down to the room at the end. Opening the sliding hatch, I peeked through and saw that Nick was awake, sitting gloomily on the edge of his bed, even his grand moustache had deflated. I unlocked the heavy door then ambled through, unfolded the small deck chair in the corner and sat down.

"How are you, Nick?" I politely asked, feeling sorry for him as he struggled to look me in the eye. "Alright to ask you questions? Not formally, but as a friend."

"Friend?" The publican quietly snorted, "All you coppers are bent."

"I want to talk about the gun. *Your* gun to be precise."

"What do you want to know? You already know it's my gun, but I didn't use it on Ben or Joseph. I found it by the backdoor when I went outside to turn on the power supply in the outhouse. I only take it with me when I head up north for hunting, last time I used the rifle was in September. It's been locked up since."

"Under lock and key?"

"That's right. Key is kept in my office in the safe."

"Does anyone know about the key?"

Nick shrugged his shoulders miserably, "Someone knows. I never took the gun out, I only put it back."

"You should have left it," I replied sternly, "It's a serious offence to interfere with a crime scene."

The publican snarled then snapped, "The gun wasn't at the crime scene! It was left outside the back door, a child could have found it. A child could have killed themselves. Would you have wanted their blood on your hands!? I thought so…I did the right thing by putting the rifle back."

"Why didn't you say you found it then!?"

Nick suddenly went quiet, "Constable Wright is a poor excuse for a policeman, he would have arrested me straight away if I said it was mine. He arrested Dan straightaway when he found a handgun in his pocket, my heart was racing at that moment I can tell you."

"Constable Wright and Nailer think you are behind the murders. Tell me you have an eyewitness, or you told someone else at the time about the gun."

"No. No-one saw me, and I didn't see…No, wait. That's not true, I did see someone. There was someone else out there in the snowstorm, a dark shadow, tall, slim, male, I think. I couldn't see who it was, but they were lingering by the hedges out front."

"Could it have been Dan?"

"Definitely not. Dan was inside with Isabelle when I popped out to turn the power back on." Nick confirmed, curling his moustache with his index finger.

"Jake?" I suggested.

"No. I remember seeing Jake lingering by the window, it was dark, but I could make out his figure."

"Simon?"

"No. This person was too tall to be Simon."

"Well, when you have an idea. Let me know, yes?"

Nick tiredly grinned, "Sure."

Quietly I left the room, then with a guilty conscience I locked the door and hung the key back up in the police house, knowing full well that Nick wasn't behind the killings. He was a bit of an idiot handling the murder weapon and putting it away without a word to anyone, but it didn't mean that he was a murderer. Without a motive he was completely in the clear, for now. The day had only thrown up two interesting facts, Joe's letter that he received on the morning of the day he died, it was vital that it was found. Secondly, this mysterious person hanging outside the pub in a snowstorm, minutes after Ben and Joe were killed, if it wasn't Dan, Jake or Simon, who could it be?

Chapter 14

For the third time the alarm went off at Gresham prison, as I reluctantly walked through the full body scanner; the officer in charge gave up on me and used a handheld metal detector over my persons. He shrugged and sighed put out,

"Can't find the cause. Most likely your belt. Gunna have to get you strip searched my man."

"Can't you just let it slide?" I asked feeling vexed, grabbing the rest of my things from the tray, "I'm a detective inspector, an insider not an outsider. Look, here's my badge."

"I don't make them rules man."

"Well find me the person who does! I have an appointment with one of the prisoners and I'm going to be late."

"Best we get to it then yeah? Just in this room here."

Seething with embarrassment I entered the small cubicle and as the man rudimentarily put it, I 'got on with it' and stood uncomfortably in the middle of the room. Fortunately, it was all over in a matter of minutes, a five penny coin was lodged in a small hole in my pocket, just out of reach from my grasp. Satisfied with the results, I was given permission to hurriedly get dressed and race to my interview, I only had a few minutes left. Rounding the corner at top speed I almost bumped into Chief Inspector Alec Bagman, who was too busy looking at his watch to notice me.

"Exactly on the dot Jones." He stated, looking up at me, "Rather pushing it fine, don't you think?"

"Sir." I dimly replied, wondering how on earth he knew my name. I knew his name, he had it engraved on a small gold name tag and pinned onto his breast pocket.

"I'll be taking you through and observing the interview," he continued importantly, heading down to the interview room at a gentle pace, "And don't worry. I won't say anything, I'm only there to observe."

I mutely agreed and walked through the door into the room, then gave the nod to the policeman on watch to temporarily leave, he departed to the cafeteria in haste. It was dim and dingy in the room, apart from the luminescent overhead lightbulb, which caused my eyes to water and my eyelids to blink rapidly. A surly man sniggered and flicked his loaned cigarette lighter a few times,

"You'll get used to it. I have."

"I'm not planning on spending the rest of my life here, unlike you." I growled back snatching the lighter from him, then sat down opposite, "So…is it Daniel now or shall I refer to your real name, Dylan."

"Whatever you like Jones. Whatever you like."

"Dylan then. Suits you, and it's what I have here on your case file."

"Fine. Glad that's sorted. To be honest, I didn't think I'd see your face again."

"Should've thought of that before you murdered more people!"

Dylan threw his head back and laughed, "I already told you Jones. I didn't kill anyone, I'm not a murderer."

"You're the only one who got away that night!" I snarled aggressively, slamming my hand down on the table, "You should've been dead along with Lisa and Harry."

"Hey! I never locked them in. I already told you a million times, the cabin-door latched itself shut!"

"You locked them in, threw yourself overboard and saved yourself, leaving them behind to die!"

"NO! NO, I DIDN'T. I fell over the side, I remember falling into the water, it was the cold, I remember the shock. Next thing, I'm awake in hospital." Dylan explained, clicking the bones in his fingers. "I loved Lisa, I could never hurt her."

"Did you still love Lisa after she dumped you for Harry?" I asked in a normal voice, subsiding into my chair.

"Yes."

"What about Isabelle? She dumped you too and started dating Joseph."

"What of it? It's her choice who she sees."

"Just saying," I casually remarked and sneered, "Funny coincidence though…Lisa dumped you and began dating Harry, now they're dead. Isabelle dumped you and began dating Joseph and now he's dead, was Isabelle supposed to be dead too?"

"NO! NO! I could never hurt Isabelle."

"She was at the bar when you apparently left for the toilets, guess you weren't banking on her leaving to sit somewhere else. Fortunately for her she did, otherwise there would be another grave to dig. And

I'm guessing Ben was an accident? Must have been hard to tell who's who in those Santa outfits."

"Come on inspector! I was *literally* in the toilets. Why won't you believe me?"

"The cameras, did you disconnect them just before the murders or much earlier?"

"What cameras? I didn't disconnect anything. What are you even talking about!?" Dylan shouted.

"You're a clever man, you managed to cancel Joe's gas and electric, took sneaky pictures of him and Zoe, vandalised his car and threatened him with a knife. I know what you're capable of, so no use trying to pull the wool over my eyes."

"I admit I did those things, but I never threatened Joe with a knife! It was in my hand when I opened the paint can and I forgot I was holding it."

"Ok. Look Dylan, let's just cut to the chase. I don't want to be in Whitehaven anymore, I want to go home. I'm fed up of all this crap, interviewing people, questioning suspects, searching for evidence. So come on Dylan, what do you say? Are you going to confess? We both know you did it. You give me a confession and go to prison, and I can pack my things tonight."

Dylan chewed his tongue for a moment and smiled maliciously to himself, "There's a flaw with your plan inspector. I didn't do it."

"OH, FOR CRYING OUT LOUD! WHAT WILL IT TAKE FOR YOU TO CONFESS!?"

A slight cough reverberated around the room, I had completely forgotten about the chief inspector lurking in the dark corner, beadily watching me with his large owl eyes. He deliberately coughed again and looked at his watch.

I instantly cleared my throat and inhaled a deep breath, "Right, Dylan. Run me through the events that happened on Saturday 10th December last year."

The prisoner exhaled, weaved his fingers together and placed them behind his head, "Where to start? I'm going to tell you everything inspector and it's going to be the complete truth and I won't hold anything back."

"Well there's a good start." I replied sarcastically, clicking my pen into action.

"I remember being late and rushing breakfast, I got to the pub just after 11am but fortunately the Santa run got postponed till 11.30am. Just before the race, Jake and Ben got into a fight about something, Ben got a bloody nose. Then, we raced, Ben cheated and won. Afterwards, there was food and drinks at the pub, ruddy awkward that was."

"Why awkward?"

"Well, we were all angry that Ben had cheated of course, even though he kept denying it. Joe kept giving me a lot of grief for being poor and for keeping Isabelle away from him. And then what next…I went toilet, Jake followed. Next thing, boom! I rushed back in and found Isabelle and Zoe under the table crying, then I saw the bodies. The lights came on, I think Nick turned them on? Then everyone panicked and the police were called."

"Did you not see Nick?"

"I was in the toilet, I already told you."

"So, you didn't see Nick head out or back in?"

"No." Dylan firmly responded, reaching for his cup of water.

"And Jake, where was he? I'm under the impression he was with you the whole time?" I thoroughly questioned, pausing my pen for a moment.

"Jake?" Dylan asked confused as he tried to remember, "He followed me into the toilets, but the lights went out and Jake at some point disappeared, I remember hearing the toilet door opening and closing. When I heard the gunshots and Isabelle screaming, I rushed back in as soon as I could. Jake, I don't know where he came from, but suddenly he was right behind me."

"Hmm. How long was it between the shots and you rushing back in?"

"About two or three minutes. I was halfway through a piss when I heard the gunshots. Jake must have gone out to try and turn on the power, then rushed back in when he heard the noise."

I grinned to myself triumphantly, "And now you're left without an eyewitness. Did you know Jake was covering your back by saying you were with him the whole time? But it's not true, you said it yourself, Jake left at some point leaving you on your own to kill again."

"I'm not a murderer," Dylan lazily drawled. "I don't own a gun and I definitely didn't kill anyone with a gun."

"What about the gun in your pocket? Did you know it was a non-firing replica?"

"Of course I did."

"Where did you get it from?"

"I can't remember, it's been sitting in my cupboard for donkey years. I keep it in case anyone tries to break into my house, you know, after The Marina Murders."

"You can't remember?!" I loudly scoffed, "You must know where you got it from! Did a friend give it to you? Or did you buy it from the black market?"

"No comment."

"Right, if that's how we're going to play it, you'll be fined for having an unlicensed gun on you at the very least. Why exactly did you take the gun with you to the Santa run?"

"I was hoping to get Joe on his own and threaten him with it."

"Why do you need to threaten him?"

"I want him to stay away from Isabelle. He's a dirty cheat, he's being seeing a girl called Zoe for the last three years, or so he says."

I pondered silently to myself, Zoe had said she had been dating Joe for the last three years, so if Dylan was telling the truth now, was he actually telling the whole truth about the murders too? I sighed and piled my notes back into my folder, "Ok Dylan. One more thing, did you see anyone outside just after the murders?"

"No. Why would I? I was inside the pub looking after Izzy."

"Right, that's all for now. I'll be seeing you soon."

"Inspector!" Dylan called out just as I was leaving and amicably asked, "When will I get out of here? I didn't kill anyone, I'm innocent. Please, you must believe me."

I stared into Dylan's face and took in the wrinkled forehead and the hollowed cheeks, he clearly wasn't eating or sleeping well, black shadows lined underneath his blue eyes. He didn't look remorseful for a crime he committed, he looked scared and confused. Not knowing how to reply to such an outright remark, I quietly closed the door and went on my way.

*

"How did it go? Interviewing the murderer." Constable Wright asked, passing me yet another weak tea with soft biscuits before sitting down at his desk.

I grimaced at the pale colour of the liquid, "Do you have any coffee?"

"Might do. I think there's some at the back," the young policeman replied but showed no effort of moving, "Did Dan, Dylan rather. Did he confess?"

"No," I sighed with fatigue, "No he didn't. And…I think he was telling the truth, I don't think he's the killer."

"What!? But he must be! He had the opportunity and the motive, unfortunately there's still his alibi Jake of course."

"Not anymore. Dan said that Jake left him in the toilets by himself."

"Well, there you go. Opportunity, motive and *no* alibi. Why are you so convinced he didn't do it?"

I shrugged and rubbed my tired eyes, "Some of his statement was the truth, I guess. If he was lying, why would he stupidly say he was on his own at the time of the murders, a liar would say I was with him, him and him. They wouldn't say, 'I was on my own in the toilets.' Do you get my meaning."

Wright sat perfectly upright in deep thought, "You know sir. You make a good point there. Was it Jake who told us he was with Dan the whole time?"

"Jake's statement should be in the file."

I rummaged through the pieces of paper and quickly found it, "Yes, Jake said he was with him the whole time. Now this is interesting, Jake said he went toilet first and Dan followed, but when I interviewed Dan, he said that he went toilet first and Jake followed."

"And? Does it matter who went first?"

"Not really. But I'm curious to know who's intentionally or unintentionally lying and why? I'm heading up to Badgers Farm and talk to Jake," I concluded and tugged my coat off the chair.

Wright jumped up ready for action, "I'll come with you. It's rather late for the farm, Jake will probably be at home, Primrose Cottage."

It was heading on for seven in the evening, I had no idea it was so late and felt rather guilty for calling round at such an hour. But we were already at the front door, and it was too late to head back now, quietly as I could I knocked, taking care not to wake up the neighbours. A disgruntled woman with puffy red eyes and a dishevelled blue dressing-gown, aggressively flung the door wide open,

"What do you want?" She hissed through gritted teeth, "I've just got Leah to sleep!"

"Oh, sorry," I apologised, rubbing my bristled chin to hide my embarrassment, "We want to talk to your husband, Jake?"

"You'll find him sprawled out on the sofa. Excuse me, that'll be the baby crying…again!"

Maisy swiftly left us lingering on the doorstep as she ran back up the stairs two at time, Constable Wright filled me in, "Leah is about three months now. They went through a hard time last year, Jake lost his job and this house which was tied in with the job. Got it back though, thanks to Ollie's forgiving heart. Maisy was close to her due date at the time, she moved in with her sister temporarily till the matter was resolved."

"Where did Jake stay?"

"With Dan. Thick as thieves those two. Shall we head inside do you think?"

I headed into the cottage first and drifted towards the living room, spying a sofa along the wall, I quietly lowered myself down and waited for Jake to say something. Jake glanced at us for a second before turning his eyes back to the television,

"Mr Erroneous, City Boy. What do you want?"

"Firstly, you can address us by our actual names. It's an offense to call a police officer by another name in an attempt to mock." Constable Wright announced importantly.

Jake chuckled to himself, "Where did you read that Mr Erroneous? In the big book of policing on page 226, paragraph 5? God, why is everything an offense with you!?"

"Get a grip Jake, we're not here to challenge you, we just want to ask some questions." I retorted, helping myself to a can of Coca-Cola on the table.

"Help yourself," Jake replied sarcastically, "And be quick with the questions. Maisy doesn't like people dithering in the house longer than necessary."

"Right. I've been to the prison today talking to your best friend Dan. Who went to the gents first that day? You or him? He also said that you left the toilets first just after the lights went out. But in your statement, you apparently never left Dan's side or even mentioned the lights going out. Why?"

Jake Byrd clicked his tongue along the roof of his mouth, "Straight to the point, I like it. Let's see, three months ago is a long time to remember something. I think I do remember the lights going out, but I don't remember leaving Dan. I'm pretty sure I stayed put. I'm pretty sure too that I went to the gents first and Dan followed."

"Are you saying that Dan is lying?"

"Look inspector. Dan has been my closest friend for five years. Then suddenly out of the blue he is dubbed a murderer with a fake identity. If he managed to conceal all that from me, from everyone, it makes him an extremely convincing liar. Don't you think?"

"Can you run through your movements leading up to the gunshots and after," Constable Wright asked, feeling rather proud of himself for coming up with such a question.

"Not really Mr Erroneous. I went toilet, then the lights went out. Gunshots were heard and Dan rushed out and I followed. Nothing more to it than that."

"Strange…in Dan's statement…"

"Thank you, Jake, for taking up your time to talk to us," I interrupted, jumping out of my seat and guided my young assistant to the door, "We'll be seeing you."

Constable Wright didn't look too pleased to be herded out of the door like a sheep, but he clammed up and let me guide him back outside. Once the front door was firmly closed, he rounded on me,

"Why did you interrupt me? I had a good thing going there!"

"Because we were there to ask him a few polite informal questions. Any more questions and it would have been an off-the-record interview." I exclaimed, opening the little gate at the end of the garden,

"Anyway. What did you think? Someone is lying. Jake or Dan?"

"I'm still convinced that Dan did it and Jake is covering his back. As long as Jake keeps saying he was with Dan, there's no way we can convict Dan for murder." Wright huffed and kicked out at a collapsed sofa lying in the front garden of next door. It looked odd and peculiar, I ran my hand over the armrest and upon closer inspection I noticed it appeared to have been slashed with a knife.

"What happened here then?" I asked, referring to the house next to the Byrd's.

"Ivy Cottage? Nothing really. Mindless vandals trashed the place the day after Ben was killed, Ben was living here at the time, came with the farming job. Ollie is put out about it, place is supposed to be a holiday rental to help bring in some extra income. He hasn't been able to fix it up properly yet."

I shone my torch through the downstairs window and swung it round the various rooms. The dining table was on its side and the chairs scattered, the armchairs had been pulled apart then moved to the centre of the room. Several photos on the wall were at an odd angle, ripped paper covered the floor, all the kitchen cupboard doors were open, and the contents smashed onto the tiled flooring. It didn't look like a mindless act of vandalism, it looked more sinister than that, someone was looking for something. But what? I looked at my assistant dreamily unwrapping a KitKat;

maybe I should keep my thoughts to myself for now. I swung my light towards the garage at the side of Primrose Cottage, the door was carelessly unlocked and made a lot of noise as I pushed it up. Nothing much to see, everything was under tarpaulin. Constable Wright ambled in and rummaged through some crates at the back,

"Sir? I thought Jake didn't get his motorbike back?"

Quietly I crept over to him and helped lift the cover off, "It's a bike alright. Do you think it's the same bike or a new one?"

"Same bike sir, it's identical. I've even got the plates written down in my notebook from when Jake reported it being stolen."

"Why didn't Jake say anything?"

"Makes you wonder what else he's not saying."

Chapter 15

The following morning, I awoke to the sound of song birds singing, and the sweet smell of hawthorn through my slightly opened window. It had been raining and the warm damp freshness of spring accompanied the bloom; after living in the city for so long I'd forgotten how beautiful the countryside could be. There was something different about today, no note pinned on my door threatening my life, no destruction in the bathroom, no surly looks from the men downstairs. In fact, everyone looked exceedingly worried as they toyed with their cups of coffee. I ordered my usual and sat down by a breakfast table in the snug,

"Very quiet today," I commented, accepting the full English that Jackie handed to me.

"Simon has gone missing, we thought you had arrested him alongside my husband." She retorted angrily and banged the brown sauce down in front of me, "Turns out that Constable Wright had no idea what I was talking about when I called him up about Simon! Speaking of my husband, when is he coming home?"

"Isn't he home yet? I thought Constable Nailer released him?"

"You thought wrong. I want him home, NOW! I can't run this place on my own."

"I'll see to it at once," I mumbled and tucked in, Jackie scoffed and marched back to the bar to take another guest's breakfast order. For someone who was usually so cheerful and full of life, it was very depressing to see her so sombre and moody. Chris Horridge glanced over in my direction before heading over with his pint, then plonked himself down next to me and nicked a piece of toast from my little toast rack.

"Miserable in here today. Don't you think?"

I subduedly nodded, "Enough to make you drink?"

"Eh? Oh, that. Pint of apple juice. My usual." Chris replied then leant closer to me and whispered, "Here, did ya hear? Simon has gone AWOL. Nobody knows where he's gone, supposed to be here last night but he wasn't. Not here this morning neither. They're worried for him, he won't answer his phone, nobody home. Jackie told Mr Erroneous, apparently, he's 'looking into it', that's what he said about them murders too. Turns out that Dan mightn't be the murderer after all, get a load of that! Anyways, must fly. Got a farmer to see about broad beans."

He unsteadily stood up on wobbly knees, plonked his empty glass down at the bar and exchanged a few words and money with the landlady. She peered at me with piercing eyes as she passed Chris his change, who pocketed the pennies then hobbled towards the pub door and opened it just as Constable Nailer walked through.

"Morning sir." He greeted me and took the last piece of toast.

"Nails," I grunted with annoyance, my stomach was still rumbling and now there was no toast to finish off my breakfast, "What brings you here? I thought we were going to meet at the station?"

"I'm setting up a small group to help search for Simon. We're due to meet here in ten minutes."

"Bit dramatic considering he's only been missing since last night from what I hear."

"This is Simon we're talking about. He wouldn't just go off without a word to anyone, it was dart finals too last night, he wouldn't miss it for the world."

"Well maybe something urgent came up," I feebly reasoned, draining my coffee, "Has he got family or close friends that live far away? Maybe he's gone to visit one of them?"

"No. Not Simon. There's only his mother down the road. All his friends are here in this village or Gresham. Something is wrong, I can feel it. I think he is dead."

My face turned red as I held back my laughter, "Simon isn't dead! Most likely he's done a bunk to avoid talking to me, he'll be back this afternoon guaranteed. And if he hasn't returned by tomorrow, I'll help you, by talking to the locals."

Constable Leon Nailer shook his head vigorously, "No. We need to look. Right now!"

Suddenly a blast of cool air whirled its way in our direction as the door burst open; Wright scanned his eyes over the heads of the locals massed together at the entrance. Spotting us in the furthest corner he rudely barged through the crowd in a desperation to reach us,

"He's not at home!" The young man exclaimed panting with exertion, "A neighbour heard him arrive from work and leave a few hours later, for the pub she reckons. He left just before she had supper, about 7pm."

"7pm?" I pondered absentmindedly, "But he never arrived at the pub though, what time was the darts?"

"7.30pm." Nailer replied, checking his notes. "Simon only lives around the corner, it would have taken him five minutes at least to walk over."

"Well, where did he go then? He can't have vanished!"

"Right, I'm off. Got to get this search party scattered to the four winds."

"If anything turns up, let me know straight away."

"Sir."

Wright whistled quietly to himself then cautiously sipped his burning hot cappuccino, "And now sir? What's our plan? Are we helping with the search?"

"No Wright," I bluntly replied, placing my fork and knife together with a clatter, "We have a threatening letter addressed to Joe to find. A mysterious man lingering outside the pub at the time of the murders to find. And talking about murders, we have a murderer to find too, I'm no longer convinced Dan is behind it. But first, we need to speak to Jake about his motorbike."

"Ok sir. No time like the present."

*

Badgers Farm was unusually quiet as we pulled up and parked by the main barn, not a single presence could be seen. All the animals were out to pasture, whilst the chickens were reclining inside their huts, bedded down in their cosy beds of straw. The dogs Jessie and Larch hearing our arrival barked and yapped, jumping up at the windows and pawed at the locked farmhouse door

"No-one's here." Constable James Wright sighed, then climbed back into the car and turned the engine on.

"Let's look first before jumping to conclusions. You check here and I'll work my way down to the fields.

"The dogs are locked in. Ollie only does that if he's out. Jake's bike isn't here either."

"Well, it wouldn't be, would it? I reckon we're the only people who knows that Jake has his bike back, I seriously doubt Maisy knows about the bike."

Feeling my last nerve twitch, I donned my loaned wellies and stormed off downhill through the field of sheep. The beasts glanced silently up at me and stared stupidly without blinking, a few trotted over in my direction and stopped just short of the path. One dared to baa loudly causing me to jump with surprise and tumble over a small rock sticking out of the turf.

Hearing a loud guffaw coming closer, I angrily jumped up and brushed myself down to hide my humiliation, then greeted the farmhand.

"Jake. I was hoping for a word."

"Not today, City Boy. Too much to do," Jake answered, scattering hay from a haybale around his feet for the lambs. "Saw you last night, didn't I? Why didn't you ask me then?"

"It's about your motorbike." I replied crossly.

"What about it?" The man simply responded, invading the direct question put before him.

"It's in your garage. I thought you had reported it stolen?"

"It was stolen but I got it back."

"How? Did you buy it back? Steal it back?"

"I got it back that's all. Just a misunderstanding."

"Unless you want me to caution you for wasting police time and take you to the station for questioning, just answer the question properly!" I growled irritably as my last nerve caved in.

Jake suddenly appeared downtrodden and tired as he rubbed his eyes wearily, "I'll make you tea."

Taken aback by his sudden kind offer of hospitality, I followed after him in absolute silence, struggling to keep up with his large strides. The farmhand unlocked the farmhouse and immediately placed the kettle on the hob, then handed Jessie and Larch a bone each and shooed them out the door.

"Do you want something to eat while we wait for the whistle?"

Dumbstruck by Jake's politeness I shook my head, "No, thank you."

A few minutes ticked by as Jake bustled about making tea for us and sandwiches for himself, then plonked himself down at the table opposite me,

"You want to know about my bike? Ben gave it back to me."

"Did you threaten him?" I questioned, pulling my notepad out to make notes.

"Not exactly. It was Mr Connolly, he's a forensic document examiner. First time I met him he turned up here asking for my signature to compare with an already signed document, declaring the sale of almost £10,000 for fifty-six sheep and six lambs to a farmer called Mark Hallum."

"Who is this Connolly? Is he a friend of Ben's?"

Jake sighed, bit his cheese and pickle sandwich, then hummed in thought, "I'll take you back to December, I think it was two or three days before the killings. Ben and Simon called me at home, they had my bike and were willing to give it back at a price."

"Were you angry?"

"Of course I was! I already used up all my savings to pay back Ollie for his sheep, even though it was nothing to do with me! Not to mention losing my job and home!"

"Couldn't you just leave it and buy another bike?"

"NO!" Jake shouted, rubbed his hands through his hair, then silently replied, "No. The bike, it was my dad's. Mum kept it for me till I was of age, she knows how much I love motorbikes and she knew I would treasure my dad's bike. I spent a lot of time and money making it new again."

I nodded understandingly, "Ok. I see your point. Continue."

"I went down there that evening with Dan and met them outside The King's Head. Then they jumped me, bound my legs and attempted to do the same to my arms. Dan didn't even help me, he just ran off to get help from elsewhere. That's when Connolly showed up. I don't know where he appeared from, but he was just suddenly there. There's something off about that fellow, he's proper creepy. Oh, you should have seen Simon and Ben's face, both white as a sheet and scared stiff!"

"Did Connolly say anything?" I enquired curiously, pausing my writing in thought.

"Yes. He asked Ben and Simon where the money was."

"What money?"

"I guess the money they made from selling the sheep, but I'm only guessing. Ben handed him a thin envelope and Connolly counted the notes. Then boy, was he mad! I don't know what went wrong, but I'm guessing the money wasn't all there. Then he found out that Ben was trying to get more money out of me by selling me my own bike! That smirk however, that Connolly gave my brother was just pure evil. He must have whispered something to him, because Ben was suddenly by my side taking off my ropes and handing me my bike."

I rubbed my forehead thoughtfully, "And again I ask, why would a forensic document examiner ask for money in such a peculiar fashion? Didn't you find it all a bit strange at the time?"

Jake firmly bobbed his head, "Oh yeah, definitely. But I got my beloved motorbike back. Dan turned up a second later with Nick and some others from the pub. Connolly, Simon and Ben scarpered in different directions and I simply went home."

"Can you describe Mr Connolly? Or better yet, are you willing to do an E-FIT?"

"Tall and lanky, short brown hair. Owl glasses. Oldish. You should really be asking Mr Erroneous, he accompanied Connolly that day he came over to ask about signatures."

"Really!? Right, I'll ask him. Thank you." I responded, zipping my coat up to the top as a heavy rain drop splattered down with a clatter onto the porch roof. "Oh, by the way, did you know Simon has gone missing?"

Jake laughed and opened the door for me, "Simon!? Nah, I wouldn't say he's missing. Probably gone off to visit a friend somewhere and forgot to mention it. He'll be back tonight."

Black clouds had astonishingly closed in with ferocious speed, making for a vast contrast from the white fluffy clouds from only an hour ago. Quickly I ran back to the car and slammed the door, just as the heavens opened and a torrential downpour descended. Jake however didn't seem bothered by the weather and stepped out calmly into the storm and headed over to the dairy. His dogs however couldn't have run back inside the farmhouse quick enough, with their tails well between their legs and whined fearfully.

"How it'd go with Jake?" Constable Wright enquired, winding his seat up from its reclined position and straightened his uniform.

"Interesting," I replied, helping myself to a mint from the glovebox, "You could have come in you know."

"I don't like Jake. He's too full of himself, lording it over everyone like he knows best! What did he have to say about the bike?"

I repeated the conversation I had with Jake, the young policeman bobbed his head continuously as he tried to understand, the picture was finally coming together.

Reaching the end of the retelling, I then asked, "Jake said you were with Connolly when he turned up here asking for a signature for comparison?"

Constable James Wright tapped his mouth with a finger, "Oh yes, now I remember that name Connolly. Mark Hallum wasn't convinced that it was Jake's signature on the document, had suspicions apparently, but Connolly soon sorted out the matter and proved it was legit."

"How did he go about it?"

"Eh? Oh, well. He had Jake sign a blank piece of paper and compared the signature with the signature on the document with a magnifying glass."

I laughed to myself and shook my head, "He's a phoney then, no forensic document examiner would ever compare signatures that way! How did you find him?"

"I didn't. Ben turned up at the station with him. You see, Mark told *Ben* that he was suspicious of the signature and *Ben* said he'll sort it out with his brother Jake. Anyway, Ben turned up with Connolly, told me about his brother Jake illegally selling sheep, and wanted me to go with Connolly to the farm to prove it. Jake didn't know that Ben was aware of his rustling scheme, that's why Ben had to go behind his back."

"And you didn't ask any questions?"

"Well, no. It all made perfect sense."

"And you just went along with it," I sighed wearily starting up the car, then mumbled, "Storm is slowing down. If you saw Connolly again, would you recognise him?"

Wright tilted his head from one side to the other, "Maybe. But I don't know where he lives or what his first name is either!"

"Call yourself a policeman," I muttered under my breath and drove down the bumpy lane cautiously.

Turning into the main road I spotted a small group of people hunting through the bushes whilst beating the hedgerow with their walking sticks, a couple of pheasants scattered in alarm along with the odd partridge. As we neared the village, we spotted Nailer deep in conversation with Jackie and a few other villagers; they were standing on the edge of a field bent over a map. Carefully I pulled over to one side and made my way over,

"Anything?"

Nails looked at me with large concerned eyes, "Possibly. Joan here thinks she saw something last night just after 7pm. She knows Simon and she swears it was him being pushed into a car by two large men, which drove off seconds later at a horrific speed. And we also found this."

Gingerly I took the sealed bag from him and stared at the contents inside, "Is this Simon's phone?"

"It's got his cards in the case. Looks like someone smashed it good with a hammer and threw it from the car window, Joan found it by the roadside."

"Simon is a builder," Constable Wright spoke up, taking the phone from me to have a look at, "Do you think it's work related? Builders use hammers all the time."

"Possibly," I replied, scouring the land with my eyes. "Unfortunately, if Simon was taken in a car, then we have very little chance of finding him. He could be anywhere in the country. Anything else? Any other leads."

Nailer shook his head dismally, "Nothing. Nothing at all."

Chapter 16

Silently I sipped my English Breakfast tea from The Little Maple with contentment, Isabelle had been good and allowed me to take my cup on the go. My assistant was happily content with his watery mixture and dunked his rock hard ginger biscuits in to soak.

"What do we do now Wright?" I solemnly asked, draining my cup.

Constable James Wright spluttered on his tea and uncomfortably snorted as the liquid went up his nostrils, "You're asking me sir? Wow…what an honour. I…um. I've been thinking about Mr Connolly, and I think I'm going to start looking for him. There's nothing we can do for Simon. And we've haven't got much to go on looking for our murderer. I reckon Connolly is going to be a big lead."

"Did you check the phone book? Internet? Villagers?"

"I'm on it now sir."

"Right. I'm going to go through Joe's possessions in the lockup at Gresham. See if I can find this letter Zoe mentioned. Meet you back here at 3pm."

*

The self-storage warehouse in Gresham lived up to its name, it was Big and Yellow, and easily spotted on my right as I zoomed down the main road. Thankfully it was quiet inside and the warehouse assistant non-hesitantly showed me to a large locker located at the other side of the building. There wasn't much to go on, his personal effects had been boxed up alongside his evening suits, a couple of expensive items had been labelled and wrapped carefully in bubble-wrap. Choosing the box nearest to me I dug in, pulling out various letters of importance and bank statements. An hour passed by quicker than I realised, and with one last box to go, I had almost given up hope, when bingo. A letter which had been crumpled up then smoothed down to fit back inside the envelope; was lodged in between the pages of an address book. Carefully I studied the envelope first, there was no name on it or marks. Unfolding the rustling page, I could just make out a few scribbly sentences, written in red ink as Zoe had said:

YOU WON'T GET RID OF ME THAT EASY! AFTER TODAY YOU'RE GOING TO WISH YOU NEVER CROSSED ME! YOU BETTER WATCH YOUR BACK OR I'LL MAKE YOUR LIFE HELL!

I wasn't in the least impressed with such a childish note, no threat of violence or any threat to kill; there was only one person who could have written it and that was Daniel. Zoe had mentioned that Dan was more verbally abusive than physical, and everyone I so far had talked to all said that he was a softy and rather pathetic. And this letter just further proved how pathetic he really was. I rummaged through the remainder of the box, some photos and letters, other memorabilia and…

"What on earth?" I uttered out loud and whipped the sheet of paper from the box.

Dear Mr Rogers,

Thank you for your kind letter, I wasn't in the least offended as you probably hoped I would be. Unfortunately, your capital still needs to be paid in full and by the end of the month as agreed.

"Et cetera, et cetera."

…if the payment isn't paid in time, life will become exceedingly unpleasant for you. Think of your loved ones,

Kind regards

Seamus Connolly

Was this the same Connolly that accompanied Wright? Connolly, the fake forensic document examiner? It was dated 23rd of November, Joe only had one week to pay up, that wasn't very long. How much did Joe owe this Mr Connolly? Hurriedly I opened the box full of bank statements and yanked out a small wedge of sheets stapled together, along with other pieces of important letters related to money. Joseph Rogers was heavily in debt, mortgaged to the hilt, various loans still unpaid, credit cards fully maxed. A bank statement from September stole my attention, a large sum of £50,000 had been deposited into his account from none other than Seamus Connolly himself. Who was this Connolly?

A rich relative, a wealthy friend, an investor, money lender? I filed the paperwork into an empty folder, including the letter from Daniel which was far from a threat as possible, if anyone had written a threatening letter it was Connolly. At least Joseph didn't have loved ones, but there was Zoe and Isabelle to consider. Why though was Joseph killed? Was Connolly behind his death? You wouldn't kill someone who owed you money…would you? Nothing made sense, hopefully Wright had found Connolly by now and was able to add to the mystery.

*

Constable James Wright placed the last tidied folder into its correct place in the filing cabinet drawer and rather proudly closed it shut. With a broad beam on his face, he sat down to his rearranged and neat desk then straightened his tie.

"Turning into the inspector's little lap dog, are we?" Nailer meanly joked and then laughed, "He's going to be so proud of you. Are you going to jump up and down when he gets back or bark with delight?"

I coughed loudly behind Nails to announce my arrival then passed round the sausage rolls, "Haven't you got some work to do Nails?"

Leon Nailer hurriedly left rather red faced, slamming the door on the way out to show his annoyance, the sound of skidding car wheels was heard. I hungrily tucked into my lunch and completely ignored that aggravating constable, how he became a police officer in the first place was beyond me.

Wright cleared his throat and stood upright with importance, "Sir. I found Connolly. He lives just down the road near the primary school. His first name is Seamus, forty-nine, single and no family."

"Good work constable. Does he have a real job other than his fake one?"

"Not sure sir. Apparently, he stays at home most days and only goes out at night."

"Definitely not a forensic document examiner then."

"Not likely sir. Shall we go and talk to him?"

"Yes. But first, hear me out." I showed the constable my findings and shared my thoughts on the case, "Quite a lot to go on. I think we can rule out Dan's silly letter and start focusing on Seamus."

Wright nodded, "Do you think Ben borrowed from him too? Remember you said, that Jake said, that Connolly said to Ben, 'Where's the money?'"

"Hmm, it would make sense. I'm thinking too that's why Ben sold the sheep, to get money to pay back Connolly. But why did Ben borrow in the first place? And why didn't Ben hand over all the money? Where's the rest of it?"

"What I want to know is why Connolly is being so secretive about being a money lender? Why pretend to be a forensics document examiner?"

"Maybe he's not a money lender?" I replied, heading back outside, "Let's go ask him…shall we?"

*

Seamus Connolly's house was positioned right opposite the school, the primary school children were having an afternoon break and were cheerfully playing outside. A little girl spotted Wright and called out loudly to the policeman, the other children stopped their play and came running to the fence. Constable James Wright glowed with pride and wandered over, overwhelmed to be placed on such a high pedestal in the children's eyes, as he emphasised the importance of his job to them. The teacher came over ringing the bell to call them back to class, and she smiled coyly in the direction of the constable then headed in herself. Feeling rather flustered, the young policeman crossed back over the road to join me.

"She's pretty, isn't she? The teacher." I stated, knocking strongly on Connolly's door, "The children are very fond of you."

"Yes…well, it's a small village sir."

"You say it's a small village and yet you've only met Connolly once and know nothing about him."

"True. Jackie mentioned he's only just moved in end of last month. This used to be the old schoolhouse," said Wright, and after a pause he added, "It's also where Dan lived."

"WHAT!? And you're only just telling me this now!"

The door opened at that precise moment, a tall thin man with the largest brown eyes I'd ever seen, placed on a rather square face; and casually wore a country squire outfit. He peered down at us and coughed dryly, "Can I help you gentlemen?"

"Mr Seamus Connolly?" I enquired, showing him my badge, "We would like to ask you some questions, if you have a moment?"

"Of course, come on in. Apologies for the boxes I've only just moved in, and the previous tenant left the place in an awful mess."

"The previous tenant being Daniel Cooper I'm told." I exclaimed glaring at Wright and sat down on a dilapidated sofa.

Connolly just stared blankly at me, "If you say so? I don't know who Daniel is."

"Don't you read the papers or go on the internet? Dan Cooper was the man arrested for the murders of Ben Byrd and Joseph Rogers." Constable Wright proclaimed. "Now, we have some questions for you."

"I'm all ears."

"How did you know Ben?" I asked, shifting my backside sideways off an uncomfortable spring.

"Tea. Inspector...Jones, was it? How about you Wright?" Connolly ambled to the kitchen and potted about with the cups, "Ben was one of my clients. I'm a money lender of sorts."

"Client? So, you loaned him some money?"

"Yes. It's what I do."

"What was the loan for?"

"Ben wanted to start up his own building trade, but he was already heavily in debt with the bank. Unfortunately, the business didn't start off that well and eventually collapsed."

"I heard it was a dodgy business that had to be forced to close, by law."

"If you say so. I'm only a money lender, I'm not interested in where the money goes as long as I get it back on time."

Constable Wright scratched his head puzzled, "When we first met, you said you were a forensics document examiner?"

Seamus Connolly chuckled and because of his dry throat it came out sounding more like a cruel cackle, "That was just a farce. It was Ben's idea, and I went along with it, he wanted to put the wind up his brother. Jake stole some sheep as you're probably fully aware, thought he got away with it, but Ben knew. Hence all the theatrics."

"Jake almost got a prison sentence because of your charade. Do you realise how serious this is?" I protested, taking the cup that Connolly passed to me.

"Jake wouldn't have gone to prison. Ben and I made sure he got bail."

"What about the money from the sheep sale? Does Jake still have it, or did he give it back to the farmer?"

"I have reason to believe that Jake still has it, Ben said that Jake gave him some but not all the money. If you want to ask someone about money, you should ask Jake. He's a very shifty character."

Wright quickly spoke up, "A few nights before the murders you demanded the money off Ben. Why did you demand the money off Ben if you knew that Jake has the rest? Why not demand the rest of the money off Jake? Apparently, you got very angry with Ben."

"Says who?" Connolly aggressively challenged, "Did Jake say so? Judging by your poker face I've guessed right."

"Ok then, moving on." I swiftly interrupted, putting a stopper to the argument, "What about Joseph? Was he one of your clients too? Only I found this threatening letter in his possession with your signature on it."

Connolly took the letter and studied it for a minute then handed it back, "Hardly threatening inspector. Merely instructing. If the money isn't paid on time, I have no choice but to harass family members and friends…that's all."

"All legit and above board, is it? Nothing illegal about your business?"

"Nothing at all Inspector Jones. Any more questions?"

"Ben's home was burgled the day after he was killed," Wright interjected, "Know anything about that?"

I took a deep breath in and watched Connolly's face intensely, burgled wouldn't have been my word choice, ransacked or destroyed would have been closer to the truth.

Seamus Connolly quietly sipped his tea, his posture completely relaxed as he calmly replied, "No. Nothing to do with me. Anything missing?"

"Not that I recall." Wright admitted.

"One more thing," I intervened, standing up to leave, "Where were you Saturday 10th December at the time of the murders?"

"Me?" Connolly asked confused, "I was at home, my old home in Gresham. And no, no-one can vouch for me unfortunately."

"So, it wasn't you hanging around outside The Fox and Rabbit at the time the gun went off?"

"Definitely not."

"Right. Thank you. We might be back to ask more questions."

"Anytime Inspector Jones. Wright."

Stepping back outside we were momentarily swallowed up in a throng of parents; come to pick up their children from school. Weaving our way through the small mass, we headed back along the river to the village centre, collecting our thoughts along the way.

"Strange man, Connolly. Don't you think?" I considered thoughtfully.

Constable Wright couldn't be quick enough to agree as he was thinking the same thing, "Very strange man for a money lender, and a very strange place for a money lender to live, he looks like he should live on an estate."

"If he is a money lender." I questioned, "Money lenders don't usually give out money to someone heavily in debt and struggling to pay back what's already owed."

The constable ignorantly continued, "He looks like he's about to join a shooting party in that get up."

"He does, doesn't he? I bet he knows everything there is to know about shotguns and rifles."

"Do you think he's telling the truth sir?" Wright thoughtfully asked.

I slowly shook my head feeling rather perplexed, "Who knows anymore who's telling the truth and who's lying. I've had enough of all these games, I think we should get everyone together and sort this mess out!"

"Including Dan?"

"Especially Dan. He's at the centre of all this!" I loudly exclaimed then breathed out exasperated, "And where the hell is Simon!? We can't have this debate without him!"

"I'll check on Nailer sir."

"Yes, do that! I want to know straight away. Stupid coward is probably hiding somewhere! Probably arranged his friends to pretend to abduct him to pull the wool over our eyes."

"Shame Ben is no more. Wherever Ben went Simon would follow and Ben was seldom one for disappearing."

"Right, I'll see you later Wright. We will meet tomorrow lunchtime in The Fox and Rabbit with *everyone* in attendance including Simon!"

Chapter 17

It was nearing on for one o'clock. With precision I straightened my tie out and tucked in my shirt that Jackie had kindly ironed; it was to be a formal meeting after all. I could hear a hullaballoo forming downstairs, cautiously I peeped out of the window and witnessed Nick ushering people out of the pub. Simon's cronies weren't too pleased to be pushed outside on a Sunday, one could be heard shouting his displeasure about missing the footie. Eventually they set off, in the direction of The King's Head most likely. The police from Gresham arrived just in time, with Dan still in handcuffs and also handcuffed to the policemen's wrists, just to make sure.

Quietly I tiptoed downstairs and observed from the staircase, Isabelle and Zoe had found a sofa and were quietly talking amongst themselves in a friendly manner. Daniel was over at the other side of the pub, surrounded by four policemen no less, and looking moodier than ever. Jake and the farmer Oliver had perched themselves onto the bar stools and were watching everyone intensely. Nick and his wife Jackie were behind the bar, Jackie was nervously wringing a tea-towel, not taking her eyes off Dan for one moment. Seamus Connolly had chosen a chair in a non-conspicuous corner and attempted to hide his face with The Times. Simon had finally made an appearance and whatever happened to him, he looked absolutely dreadful. His face had clearly taken a good beating, he was almost unrecognisable; with probably more bruises on his persons as he shifted himself uncomfortably on the hard chair. Chris Horridge…actually, why was Chris here? Clearly, he didn't have anything to contribute, he was only here for the bangers and mash and tucked in wholeheartedly. Perhaps Wright thought he would be of some use? And lastly a woman with dark brown hair once possibly dyed red, I recognised her face, but from where?

A voice sounded behind me, "All here sir. We even found Simon sir."

"I noticed. Good job Wright," I congratulated and patted him on the back, "Just in time too. Where did you find him?"

"At home. His neighbour saw him entering his home about ten last night. I went by this morning and knocked on his door."

"Did he say where he was or where he'd been or who he was with?"

"Nothing. He just said see you later and closed the door in my face."

"Right," I simply replied, my eyes fixed on the people in the pub, "Got all the evidence?"

"Yes sir."

"Good man. Alright, let's see what they have to say for themselves."

Superiorly I stepped over the void and entered the main area of the pub, everyone immediately stopped their idle chatter to stare at me, apart from Chris who was happily finishing off a crumble.

"Afternoon everyone. We all know why we're here and I believe one of you, in this room, murdered Ben Byrd and Joseph Rogers in cold blood." I began importantly and dramatically, "And to keep this simple we will use Dan's real name, Dylan. I assume we all know each other but just to make sure, can you all introduce yourselves one by one please."

There was silence as everyone introduced themselves one by one, a few people showed genuine surprise, whilst the rest just scowled. I was also taken by surprise, for the woman next to me was none other than Margaret Taylor, Lisa's mother and the same woman who knew Dan's real name to be Dylan.

"Ok," I concluded and began to pace up and down in thought. "Where to begin. When I first came to Whitehaven, I thought this would be just another open and shut case. Turns out to be more, much more than that. And I hate to have to admit it…but actually…I don't think Dylan is the murderer."

A loud cry of protest and cheers echoed around the pub, Margaret stood up first to voice her opinion, "You are wrong inspector, and you know it. He murdered my daughter. He was there on the night she was killed. He locked her in the cabin with her boyfriend Harry and jumped off the boat into the water to save himself from the flames. All this pretence that he can't remember is just that! Pretence!"

Dylan jumped up aggressively, taking the policeman by his side by surprise and pulled him over by accident, "I DIDN'T KILL LISA OR HARRY! I TOLD YOU THOUSANDS OF TIMES...YOU STUPID COW!"

A slight cough alerted my attention to the girls sat on the sofa, Isabelle quietly asked with her hand raised, "Sorry. Is it just me or does no one else know what's going on?"

"You should be asking you murdering boyfriend honey," Margaret snapped, eyeing Isabelle judgementally, "He's the one holding all the cards here!"

"He's not my boyfriend!"

"Oh, right yeah, sorry. Your boyfriend is the one who got murdered, Joseph right?"

"HE'S *MY* BOYFRIEND...was my boyfriend." Zoe loudly exclaimed standing up, "Joe made a stupid mistake dating Izzy, but it was just that...a mistake and nothing else."

"Glad we've got that sorted," I announced abruptly, taking over once more, "For those that don't know. Five years ago, I was on a case called The Marina Murders, in my home town of St Heliers. Dylan with his friends Lisa, Harry and Nathan were celebrating Nathan's 30th on Harry's boat. At some point Nathan left the party and the boat left the marina and went out to sea. Then the boat caught fire, possibly by the many candles. By the time the services arrived, the boat was almost destroyed. Dylan was found floating about at sea in a rubber dinghy, Harry and Lisa were found dead in the cabin with the door cabin-door latched from the outside."

"By HIM!" Lisa's mother shouted, pointing her finger at Dylan and glared at him suspiciously.

"Right. Moving on. Fast forward five years, Dylan Worthy has now a new life, he is now called Daniel Cooper., He's got a new girl called Isabelle and he is a gardener by trades and living in Whitehaven. It is now Saturday 10th December, the Santa Dash. Nick and Jackie hold this event every year to remember their son George, correct? Ok, so, everyone raced, and I understand that Ben cheated? And Jake and Ben had an argument at the beginning of the race over some sheep? Anyone want to confirm or elaborate on that?"

"It's pretty much what I told you inspector," Jake drawled, resting his elbows on the bar behind him, "Ben was going to admit to the rustling if I won the race, but if *he* won the race then *I* would be the one admitting. Ben cheated the race and won, like I said."

A slight gasp reverberated around the room.

"Fine. But you didn't actually admit to stealing the sheep, did you? I'm confused at this point, did Ben steal the sheep or did you? Mr Seamus Connolly says it was you who stole the sheep because Ben said so."

"Ben said so," Jake scoffed, rolling his eyes.

"Ben also hired Seamus to check a signature from you for comparison, Ben knew you stole the sheep, and he didn't want you to get away with it."

"If it was me inspector who stole the sheep, where's the money!?"

Ollie quietly piped up, "You did manage to pay me back."

"With my savings!" Jake proclaimed irritably. "You should really be asking how *Ben* came into so much money!"

"It's come to my understanding that you gave your brother the money after selling the sheep." Seamus Connolly suddenly announced.

"Why on earth would I give my dope of a brother ten grand in money?"

"So he could pay me back."

Jake cruelly laughed, "God. Why does no one believe it's all Ben? Ben stole the sheep for money, money to apparently pay you back Seamus. I never sold the sheep, why would I? I don't need the money, I have or had plenty in my bank, and I would never go behind my employer's back. I'm an honest worker."

"He does make a point there." I concluded sitting down on a bar stool at the far end of the bar, "I next figured that Ben borrowed from you Seamus, so he and Simon could start up their building company. Unfortunately, it went bust after police found they were operating illegally. It's been a struggle for Ben, but when he finally found a way to get money from rustling sheep to pay you back. Why didn't he? Where did the money go?"

"Horses." Jake calmly interrupted before Seamus Connolly could reply, "I found betting slips in his house."

"It was you who trashed his house?" I questioned.

"No. I simply found the slips on the table."

"Then it was you Seamus who trashed Ben's house, looking for the rest of the money. You threatened Ben for the money a few nights before, don't deny it. And when Ben didn't cough up the right amount, you killed him, then went to his house to look for the rest. You didn't know that Ben bet most of your money away on the horses, did you?"

"Fun story inspector," Seamus Connolly coolly replied, crossing his legs, "I threatened him yes. But I didn't kill him, why would I kill someone who owed me money?"

"And the house?"

"Fine. I admit I sent my boys to Ben's house to find the rest of the money, I didn't know he gambled it away."

"Ha!" Constable James Wright exclaimed as he suddenly just realised something and it clicked in his head, "I got it! You're a loan shark."

I rolled my eyes with annoyance for I had already figured that out too, "Yes Wright. He's a loan shark, well spotted. Right. After the race then what happened? Dylan and Joseph had an argument I believe, what was it really about Dylan? You said Joe wanted you to feel small and guilty for keeping Isabelle to yourself, was it about that? Or was it about this here letter? Did Joe know it was you who pushed it through his door?"

Constable James Wright importantly handed Dylan the note concealed in a plastic sealed wallet, waited for a moment, then snatched it back and placed it with the rest of the evidence.

Dylan blanked out for a second to think, "I won't deny I wrote it. But I don't remember posting it. Me and Joe got into a scrap one night over some photos, I wrote the letter in anger but regretted it the next day. I was going to rip it up, but I couldn't find it."

Isabelle meekly coughed, everyone whirled round to look at her, she blushed and explained, "It was me…Dan. Dylan, sorry. Have to get used to that. I posted it inspector. I read the letter, and I knew that Dylan wouldn't send it. I was furious with Joe for hurting Dylan, I wanted to get back at him too, on Dylan's behalf that is."

Dylan and Isabelle exchanged a small loving smile, each relieved that the invisible string connecting their hearts was still intact, despite being a little frayed in places. Their eyes locked and neither looked away, the rest of the people in the room could feel the love vibration between them.

"Now." I continued, breaking up the atmosphere as I reached for my next piece of evidence, "We have two guns. One replica. One rifle. Dylan, you didn't say where the replica came from?"

Dylan looked at me baffled, "I told you already. It's been in my cupboard for like, forever."

"Ok then. And this rifle, which you already said is yours, Nick?"

The publican looked up at me, twirling his moustache as he amicably nodded, "Hmm. I already told you it's mine. But I haven't used it in ages, it's usually in my cellar."

"Yes. The cellar. I've just been down there…did you know? It's very easy to get down into your cellar without being seen. I already found the key in an open safe, only took me a minute to open the rifle cabinet."

Nick suddenly looked sheepish and tried to hide his face by looking down, "Right."

"Now. We just need to figure out who used it. Since everyone and anyone had access to your rifle and only your prints were found on it Nick; regrettably we can't use your gun anymore as evidence. You said you found it by the back door? Correct?"

Nick Lawson glumly nodded, "Just after the shootings. I went out to turn on the electrics."

"And you didn't pass anyone in the corridor?"

"That's right. But I did see someone outside."

"But not Jake and Dylan because they were inside. Not Simon either because you said it was someone tall and thin…Seamus…stand up for me will you."

Mr Connolly sneered with displeasure, then quietly raised himself up with his chin held high.

"This him?" I just as quietly asked as yet another hush fell about the room as everyone stared bulge-eyed at Seamus.

Nick suddenly trembled with excitement and jumped up pointing, "Yes! It's him! I'm pretty sure it is, he's the right height and size. Although I only saw his silhouette."

"Mr Connolly. Care to explain why you were outside at the time of the shootings?"

"It wasn't me," Seamus Connolly replied, sitting back down and returned to his crossword puzzle.

"Jake? What do you think?"

Jake looked up at me in alarm, "Why are you asking me for? I was in the toilets the whole time."

"Ah yes. The toilets. The toilets which you never left. Your friend Dylan however says otherwise."

"He's wrong."

"Dylan?" I prompted inquisitively, staring at the prisoner in cuffs and waited for his answer.

Dylan shrugged, "I got it wrong then. I thought it was Jake I heard leaving. I thought it was only me and him in the gents that night, there must have been someone else there too."

"And Simon? Where were you that night? Did you see anything or anyone?"

Another silence reverberated as everyone turned to look at Simon, Simon twiddled with his ring on his baby finger as he contemplated an answer.

"I left the bar. Seconds before the shooting."

"Liar," Zoe scoffed and explained, "The moment the lights went out I saw you running into the backroom and then I saw you running out of the front door a few minutes later. The shooting literally happened a second after you left the pub.

"So, Zoe can vouch for your whereabouts Simon, that's good news for you, because it's physically impossible to arm yourself and take fire all within a second. Now, care to explain why you were in the backroom or shall I presume you were stealing?" I fiercely questioned, however receiving no answer I ploughed on, "However, I suppose if you *did* steal something, Nick and Jackie would've reported it. So, I assume you left empty handed? I also assume you made a habit of stealing to pay back Seamus? You were simply helping Ben pay off his debt to this here loan shark…How am I doing so far?"

Simon didn't respond and just humbly nodded, the ring on his finger had got stuck and was sinking into his fleshy skin.

"Now," I continued, ignoring the silence, "Zoe said you ran out the front door seconds before the shootings happened. Did you see anyone or anything unusual?"

"No." Simon mumbled, staring at his feet and wishing that the ground would swallow him up.

"Simon, hear me out. There were possibly four people outside at the time of the murders, Jake, Nick, Seamus and yourself. You must have seen someone!"

"Yes," Simon whispered to himself, as everyone leaned forward straining their ears as hard as possible to hear him, "I saw a man behind the hedge with a gun, he threw it away and ran to the back of the pub."

"You could have told us this earlier Simon! You have deliberately withheld vital information and obstructed this case!" Constable James Wright retorted slamming his pen down, he turned to Simon and crossly interrogated him. "What did you do then? Did you pick up the gun and put it by the back door for Nick to find?"

"Not me…him. Connolly."

"WHAT!? YOU LIAR!" Seamus Connolly bellowed, leaping up in fury with his face blazing and his fists ready, "I WASN'T THERE THAT NIGHT! WHAT ARE YOU PLAYING AT SIMON!? IS THIS PAY BACK FOR…"

"For what Mr Connolly?" I coolly interrupted, stopping the ferocious man mid-sentence who immediately paled and slumped back in his chair. "Pay back for what? It was your boys, wasn't it? Kidnapping Simon and showing him what happens when you don't pay up in time!? Now, tell me…what did Simon see? Did he see you kill Ben Byrd and Joe Rogers?"

Seamus had simmered down considerably and regained his calm pose as the colour came back to his cheeks, "No. It wasn't me, I didn't kill anyone. I simply picked up the gun and placed it by the back door…that's all."

"That's all? For someone who *supposedly* wasn't there that night, you're now admitting you moved the gun!? Why? Why did you move the gun?"

"No comment."

"It's not an interview room for crying out loud!" I shouted, banging my fist down on the table, "Did you see *anyone* other than Simon when you put the gun by the back door? Did you see Dylan and Jake leave the toilets? Did you see Nick by the outhouse?"

"I didn't dally as you can imagine, I made a quick retreat back to my car. But I did see Dylan running down the corridor into the heart of the pub."

"Dylan? But not Jake?"

"That's correct."

"I WAS RIGHT NEXT TO HIM YOU BLIND DOPE!" Jake yelled, leaping up and grabbed Seamus by the collar, tightening his grip as he stared him straight in the eye and growled, "I was with Dylan the whole time…you know it's true! Why don't you say it!? What have you to gain by LYING!?"

Dylan coughed slightly to draw attention to himself, "Inspector, Jake was with me. When I rushed out of the toilets, he was there right behind me. Connolly *is* lying, Jake was right next to me when we went back into the pub, there's no way that Connolly didn't see him."

Jake backed away and waited for Connolly's response, Seamus Connolly straightened his shirt and tucked it back in, "I must have been mistaken then."

"Mistaken?" Constable Wright asked with confusion, "What…were you drunk? How many people did you see running down that corridor? One or two?"

"I thought one at the time. But it could've been two."

I wearily sighed, "Ok. I'm in need of a coffee break. Wright, Nailer, with me. We're going to talk this out in the snug. We'll be back in twenty."

Chapter 18

With our coffee cups in hand to restore our minds and a plateful of biscuits to replenish our stomachs, we dived straight back into the case at hand. Constable Wright had written up pages of notes and I quickly skimmed through it all, there were lots of crossed out lines and question-marks. I scratched my head in bewilderment and opened the meeting,

"Ok. We need to rearrange our timeline of events. Wright, do you want to take over this bit since it's your writing?"

"Yes sir," Wright enthusiastically replied, "It's all there written down. 3.30pm is roughly when the murders happened. Leading up to that, we have Ben,

Jake, Dan or Dylan, Simon, Izzy and Zoe. The men lingered by the bar whilst the girls sat down."

"I think we can rule the girls out sir." Nailer intervened, crushing his paper cup and tossing it in the bin.

"Not yet. Everyone's a suspect, and we haven't properly interviewed the girls together." I carefully explained, "Go on Wright."

"Sir," said Wright and continued, "Next up, Dylan and Jake went toilet. The lights went out. Jake left the toilets, where did he go? Shots were heard. Dylan and Jake rushed back in, Nick then left to turn on the power. We've established that Connolly and Simon were also outside at the time of the shooting, possibly Jake. Connolly admitted he left the gun by the back door after the shooting; Nick found the gun, realised it was his and returned it to the cellar."

"Ok. Let's establish everyone's movements. Zoe and Isabelle were on the couch, yes? But we'll ask again to make sure. Dylan was on his own in the toilets, but Connolly only saw him the once and that was when he was returning to the heart of the pub. It doesn't seem likely that Dylan was outside, there's too many people outside traipsing about, someone would have seen Dylan."

"True," Nailer admitted and bobbed his head in agreement, "But those people traipsing about as you put it, are firstly Simon who is a thief, Seamus who is a loan shark, and Nick who is simply turning back on the power. Simon and Seamus only admitted they were outside when they came under pressure."

"I thought Seamus scarpered quickly? Why did Nick see him lingering out by the front long after the shootings?" Constable Wright considered, rubbing his chin as he pondered.

"Hmm," I replied, nodding my head in agreement, "An excellent point Wright, well done. Simon didn't kill anyone, not enough time."

"Do you think Seamus killed them sir?"

"Maybe…but loan sharks don't usually kill off their clients, they maim and injure. They want their money back, don't they? They won't get their money back off a dead person."

"Jake? He still hasn't confirmed where he was at the time. We know where he was before the lights went out and after the shootings took place, but not in between."

Nailer scratched his bristly cheek, "I don't like Jake. A convulsive liar with a horrific temper, I wonder if he's like that at home?"

"He's very sure of himself," I agreed, suddenly I had a lightbulb moment, causing me to accidently curse, "Damn! The bike! I'll be back in a minute, I need to talk to Maisy."

"What about them in the pub sir?" Wright exclaimed surprised.

"Give them cake Wright. Just…you know…roll with it." I replied tugging on my coat and speedily left by the back.

Nails chuckled and helped himself to a wedge of chocolate cake, "Sounds like something that Elvis P would say!"

*

Pressing my foot down on the accelerator and much harder than necessary, I ploughed my bruised car up the bumpy track, the wheels banged and groaned with every pothole. Fortunately, it was late afternoon which must mean that someone should be home, stepping up to the front door I knocked quietly, taking care not to wake Leah this time. The door opened slowly and subtly, Jake's wife looked at me curiously as she tried to remember my face,

"Yes?"

"Maisy. D.I Jones. I was up here the other week." I replied and immediately saw her face light up in recognition, "Is now a good time to talk?"

Maisy waved an arm into her house and welcomed me in, "Of course. Leah is asleep and I'm just finishing off the kitchen."

I followed her into the house and sat down on a chair in the corner of the living room, "Are you moving? Or are you still unpacking since you moved back in?"

"We're moving." She announced with a large smile on her radiant face, "We don't want to be here anymore, we've had enough of Whitehaven. Jake has been offered a new job in Scotland, he starts next week."

"What about Jake's mother Rita?"

"All sorted, she moved into an old peoples home last weekend. Jake used his savings to secure her a room, now we just pay monthly on the rest. It was so easy I still can't believe it!"

I was thoroughly confused and stunned, "Savings? I thought Jake emptied out the account paying back Ollie?"

"Oh that, yes, he cleared out the savings. I was furious when he told me, but he fixed the problem and that's all that matters." Maisy explained, wrapping a mug in bubble-wrap. "He managed to fill up the pot again full to bursting."

"How did he manage to do that in such little time?"

"I didn't ask. I guess I don't want to know. We're no longer poor and struggling and that's all that matters."

"Maisy. I need to ask you something. Did you know that Jake got his bike back?"

Jake's wife sighed fatigued, "Yes. I know about the bike. He got it back a few days before his brother got killed."

"Did he say how he got it back?"

"He said Ben gave it to him."

"Do you want to elaborate on that for me?" I gently asked, helping her with the plates.

"I don't know, I wasn't there that night. All I know is that Dan and Jake had arranged to meet with Ben and Simon. I know something happened that night, talk of the village is that Ben and Simon were going to throw Jake into the lake."

"But they didn't."

"No. No, they didn't."

"Can I head outside to look at the bike again?"

Maisy casually bobbed her head, "Sure. Why not?"

Knowing that time was of the essence, I quickly headed over to the garage, surprisingly the bike was still there. The machine was completely intact, nothing wrong with the motorbike at all, in fact it even looked cleaner than before. I sighed frustratingly to myself as I knew my theory had gone straight out the window. Feeling disgruntled, I started pulling down boxes near to me and rummaged through, nothing of interest to be found anywhere which was hardly surprising. A toolbox on the workbench lay carelessly open, I ran my fingers over the catch and was just about to close it when I noticed something peculiar. Two pieces of frayed rope knotted tightly together, alongside some duct-tape with what looked like moustache hair stuck to it. Carefully I gloved my hands and bagged the evidence, smugly I grinned to myself, this is exactly what I needed. Suddenly a long human shadow appeared next to mine, I jumped around and was relieved to see it was only Maisy.

I showed her my encased findings, "Do you know anything about this?"

Maisy's face turned pale with shock, eventually she silently stuttered, "No, I don't. I didn't even realise we had duct-tape."

"You *do* know what I'm suggesting, don't you? Did you hear anything the night Simon got kidnapped? Come on Maisy, what aren't you telling me?"

Jake's wife struggled to reply and when she did, she was inconsolable, tears poured down her face in an endless stream. About five minutes later she dabbed her wet face with her tea-towel, "I'm sorry I lied. I did see them. These men, I don't know them. But Jake did, he was waiting for them by the garage. They had Simon bound and gagged. Then they shut the door, so I don't know what happened next. Jake went out the next morning to the farm, so I went down to the garage, just to see if Simon was still there."

"And was he?"

"No. His ropes had been cut, he was gone."

"Has Jake been acting strangely the last few months?"

"Do you mean sneaking off at night? Coming into a lot of money? Bruised knuckles from working on the farm? That sort of strange?"

"Yes, exactly that. It confirms my suspicions. Thank you."

A second later I found myself racing back towards The Fox and Rabbit, it was so quiet inside I immediately grew worried, but Constable Wright soon put my mind at ease. Most of them had taken to playing with a deck of cards, whilst the ladies had reclined to the sofa to gossip about the latest trend. Only Dylan looked fed up, he was still handcuffed to the policemen and could only observe from the other side of the room where he was sat.

"Got everything you needed sir?" Constable James Wright asked, stifling a bored yawn as he followed me into the snug.

"In a way. Send Jake in will you…actually no…send in Seamus first. I need to know something from him first."

Seizing a few moments spare, I delved into the coffee station and poured myself a cup, complete with biscuits on the side. Nailer looked up from his newspaper and noticing my arrival, grunted and folded the paper away before sitting down next to me.

Seamus Connolly glided through into the snug and sat down promptly in the chair opposite,

"Inspector."

"Connolly. I think I know why you moved the gun. You saw Jake kill his brother and Joseph in cold blood. I still haven't figured out why you were outside at the time, I can only assume you were waiting for someone? You wiped the gun then placed it by the back door, hoping that someone stupid enough will remove the gun from the crime scene. Next, I figured you blackmailed Jake to work for you in order for your silence. Was Jake's first assignment to get back the money that Ben kept? Followed up by kidnapping Simon, in an attempt to scare him into fully paying? It's the only plausible answer, Jake is the only one here who cannot verify his movements at the exact time of the murder. I know where he was before and after the murder but not in between."

"What do you want me to say?"

"Say yes."

"Fine. Yes…yes to everything. Everything you know is true."

"Did he just…!?" Constable Leon Nailer spluttered, accidently knocking his hot drink over.

I stood proudly upright and grinned with delight as I read Connolly his rights, "Nails, you and Wright know what to do. I'll meet you at Gresham prison."

Constable Wright had positioned himself next to the bar and was watching everyone with piercing eyes, making note of every movement and every conversation. Nailer walked through and pulled the young constable to one side and explained the turn of events. Wright was so shocked he promptly slipped off the bar that he was leaning on, then loudly whispered,

"You sure!?"

Nailer nodded his head towards the crowd that had suddenly stopped their talking to look at the policemen. Nails patted Wright on the shoulder, "You can do this."

Constable James Wright fumbled with his notebook for a moment whilst he gathered himself, then with his heart beating hard and fast against his chest, he ambled slowly across the room. Stopping in front of the group he exhaled a quick breath,

"Jake Byrd. I'm arresting you for the murders of Ben Byrd and Joseph Rogers. You do not have to say anything, but it may harm your defence if you do not mention when questioned something which you later rely on in court. Anything you do say may be given in evidence. Do you understand?"

No-one moved. No-one talked. No-one could take their eyes off Jake. Jake quietly raised himself up with his fists together in quiet submission, Nailer stepped forward and slapped the cuffs on. The two policemen guided Jake out of the pub and placed him in the back of the police car.

Chapter 19

Jake accepted his cup of water without even so much as a thank you, he gulped it all back and held the cup out in his hand as a gesture, asking for more. I uncomfortably watched him as he rested his head on the table, it didn't feel right to interrogate and dub him a murderer. True we didn't always see eye to eye, but despite the grouchiness, there was a kinder side to Jake, lurking just under the skin. My faithful assistant Constable James Wright entered the room and switched on the tape, he uttered our names for the tape before continuing,

"Jake Byrd. You've got some explaining to do."

Jake sneered at the policeman, "Mr Erroneous. I don't have to explain anything to you."

"In these circumstances I think it's wise that you do. You're being charged with murder!"

With so many questions to ask I quickly jumped in, "Jake. Tell me, why did you kill your brother and Joe? That's the only thing we haven't established yet, was it anger, resentment, revenge?"

Jake guffawed loudly and kept on laughing to mask his worst fears, the jig was up and life as he knew it was over.

Constable Wright crossly folded his arms and rolled his eyes then drawled, "It's no laughing matter."

Jake stopped his laughter and stared eerily and directly at him, "No, you're right. Yes, it was all three really, anger, resentment and revenge. Ben just took it too far this time, too far. I had an opportunity, and I took it."

"You must have planned it though?" I inquired baffled.

"No, I didn't actually. But I knew about Nick's gun in the cellar, everyone knew about that! I passed by the cellar on the way to the toilet, then to my surprise the lights went out. I mean it's happened before a few times, so it wasn't really a surprise as such. I had been visualising such a moment for ages you see, I had a dream for the future where Ben didn't exist in it. I used the cover of darkness to grab the gun, I ran out to the front, quickly killed my brother and ran back in. Nick's cameras don't have night-vision so I thought I could get away with it."

"The cameras were disconnected at the time Jake. And you're wrong about the night-vision, Nick had new cameras installed last year."

"News to me."

"Talk to me about the bike. It was Seamus Connolly who gave you the bike back wasn't it? Not Ben. Did you know that Ben had loaned from Seamus?"

"I didn't know, but I suspected he loaned from someone. Ten grand is a lot of money, Ben has stolen before to make ends meet, but not that much. It's only been petty stuff for hand-to-mouth pocket money. I knew he borrowed from the bank to set up his building trade, he even wanted to borrow from me at one point. I always said no. Then suddenly his business took off, expensive material was bought, ample customers and he also hired a lot of workers to work for him."

I flicked through my notes to confirm, "Tell me what happened the night you arranged to meet with Ben about your bike. The truth this time please."

Jake itched his forehead then pulled at a loose hair, "Ok. I suppose there's no harm. Now that you know Connolly is also up to his neck in it! Ben called me offering to give me back my bike and he jumped me and tied me down, that much is true, also it's true that Dan ran away. I told Ben that I knew he had borrowed from someone, and that I knew why he stole the sheep, to pay back that someone. Ben admitted it right there and then, cocky git. Simon decided to call up that someone, enter stage right Mr Seamus Connolly. Unfortunately for Ben and Simon, Seamus wasn't best pleased to be called up over such a trifle matter, he thought Simon had called him over so he could hand him the money. Anyway, Seamus took the little money that Ben gave him and demanded the rest, but my stupid brother didn't have the rest. And do you know what Ben said…!?"

"What?" I questioned intrigued to know.

"He said that *I* will pay the rest, with my money! I already spent all my savings paying back Ollie! I didn't have any more to give!"

"Then what happened?"

"Seamus Connolly untied my ropes and helped me up. Then he gave me my bike back and said, 'Pay day is set for the end of the month. Either you pay or someone you love will.' Seamus left after that, just before Dan returned with Nick and friends. Ben and Simon didn't hang around any longer and quickly left, so I too went home."

"I bet that made you mad when Connolly told *you* to pay up."

Jake snarled aggressively and crushed the plastic cup in his hand, "You think!?"

"Ben asked for it though, didn't he?" Constable Wright interjected, "He got you fired then took over the job himself, made you homeless, made you skint and now got you in trouble with a loan shark. Your brother Ben is nothing but trouble!"

The farmhand smiled cruelly, "Nicely put Mr Erroneous. Very nice. You understand why I killed him then. My wife has been through so much thanks to Ben. Being made homeless a week before her due date, hardly any money left in the accounts, I had no job which added to her stress. I killed my brother to save my wife. I got my job and home back the very next day."

"At a high price though," I reluctantly pointed out, "How will Maisy cope with you in jail or Leah? Did you even think about your baby?"

"I did. They're both better off without Ben in their lives. Maisy knew it was me by the way, she's always known. She's moving in officially with her sister until she sorts herself out, the rest of the stuff will be sold so she'll have some money put by. I gave back all the dirty money that Seamus gave me. Connolly is bent, paying me to do his dirty work, when my dirty work involved retrieving the money that Ben and Simon owed."

"Ah yes. I was just coming round to that. Seamus Connolly saw you kill Ben and Joe, is that right?"

Jake quietly nodded as he attempted to unsquash his cup, "I didn't know he saw me. I was in a rush, I didn't know how much time I had."

"We think he was standing outside waiting for someone. Was that you?" I inquired.

"No. I thought I got away with it because I bumped into Dan on the way back. It was only when Seamus

Connolly came knocking on my door the next day, I realised I was seen."

"Right. Dan or Dylan as we're now calling him. He risked himself a prison sentence by saying he was on his own in the toilets. The thing is though, I was so hellbent on convicting Dylan that I failed to realise that you too had no alibi. There was Daniel facing a murder charge and you living your life, knowing full well that he was innocent, and you were guilty. Where was your conscience at the time?"

"I didn't want to think about it…so I simply didn't."

"And Joe, why did you kill him?"

"Accident. My aim was slightly off."

"So, you tried again," Wright concluded unimpressed, "You could have killed a lot of people just to get to Ben. Luckily Simon had left, and the girls had decided to sit down on the sofa."

Realising an important factor, I chuckled quietly to myself, "You idiot Jones! That's why Simon ran to the backroom. He was going to take the charity money raised that day and pass it to Connolly outside. Unfortunately for Simon, Jackie knew about his sticky fingers and locked the money away in her own personal safe upstairs. She told me as much herself. It must have been Simon disconnecting the cameras and arranging a timed blackout…3.30pm exactly, wasn't it?"

Jake rubbed his chin in thought, "It does make sense."

"Yes, it does," I mutually agreed, "Because Seamus Connolly wasn't happy with Simon's performance, was he? And I bet he wasn't too happy with you either, killing off two of his clients before they could pay up. That's why Connolly used you because he had a hold over you, you had no choice in the matter. You had to do his bidding or face serious jail time or your loved ones getting hurt. I reckon he made you go through Ben's house, looking for the remainder of the money made from the sheep sale. And when you couldn't find it, he made you kidnap Simon and hold him hostage in your garage."

Jake gently scoffed, his ego thoroughly bruised, "I only opened Ben's door. When it was a holiday home Ollie entrusted me to look after the place and entrusted me with the key. Connolly's men were the ones who smashed the place up, I knew they wouldn't find anything though because of the betting slips. And I had to lend them the use of the garage, it was the only place where they could keep Simon hostage."

"How did Simon escape? Was it you?" Constable Wright quizzed.

"Yes. I heard you were looking for him, it was only a matter of time till you found him in my garage."

I stood up and patted my papers together, "I think that rather concludes everything. Unless you have anything else to add?"

Jake silently shook his head, it was all over, there was nothing left to say.

*

Closing my packed suitcase and pushing back in the remainder of the clothes that were sticking out, I zipped it up with a forceful flourish. I sat for a second on the edge of the bed, staring at the little room which I had become accustomed to, I wouldn't be missing this place that's for sure. Banging the bedroom door into the cupboard one last time, I squeezed the case out through the gap, then myself, and quietly closed the door. It was rather a surprise to find so many people downstairs, mostly finishing their breakfast, whilst others had simple come to say goodbye. Chris Horridge was the first to wish me well,

"Goodbye, is it? Good job catching the killer. Good job."

I warmly shook the elderly man's hand and paid for his habitual pint of apple juice, "See you, Chris."

Dylan noticed my presence at the same time I noticed him, he still wore his weary look, but his eyes were a lot brighter. Isabelle had cosied up into the nook of his arm and rested her head onto his shoulder, everything explained with no words needed. Constable James Wright took his helmet off and bobbed his head,

"Well done sir. We got him."

I rested my hand heavily on his shoulder, "Yes, we did. You make a fine police officer James Wright. Regards to Nails."

Nick picked up my suitcase then headed out to my car, ramming the case with unnecessary force into the boot. Jackie gently placed my coat on the backseat along with my other bits and pieces. I held out my hand to the publican,

"No hard feelings?"

"None at all. Be sure to come back and visit."

I snorted softly and tilted my head, I wasn't thinking of coming back to Whitehaven anytime soon. Instead, I politely replied, "Sure."

Dylan came out to see us off, holding tightly to Isabelle's hand as if to say he would never let her go again. I glanced at him briefly, my instincts still told me that it was Dylan that night who shut the cabin door on the boat, but with no way to prove it, I had no choice but to let him go his own way.

*

Friday 13th October 2017

A cold night had settled down on the marina, thick clouds covered the night sky and shut out the moon. Hardly any light was visible, safe for the small pinpricks from the lamps along the marina wall and the bright lights from the Maid of Splendour. A wild drunken party was taking place, music blared from the speakers positioned on the top deck, and paper streamers were carelessly thrown about. One of the neighbours slammed their door to show their discontent but to no avail, instead the police were called, the speakers abruptly turned off and the place suddenly silenced. The party was officially over, and the police soon were on their way to attend another out of control party.

"Who do the police think they are!?" Lisa demanded, lighting a cigarette. "Party poopers!"

Harry took the cigarette from her and inhaled deeply, "What now?"

Dylan shrugged his shoulders in defeat, "God knows. We're too drunk to be allowed in any bars or clubs."

"I think we should just head off home," said Nathan, standing up unsteadily onto his feet. "It's been a great 30th! You guys are the best. Cricket on Sunday Dylan, don't forget!"

Cries of protest were heard as the others attempted to pull him back down into his deckchair, but Nathan shrugged them off with a laugh and clambered down the ladder onto the boardwalk. Lisa moodily watched him from the top deck, then threw herself down on some cushions laying around the portside as the other two men joined her.

"This is sooo boring!" she sighed, pulling a blanket up to her chin and shivered. Dylan snuggled up to her

and rubbed her arms to help her warm up whilst Harry watched intensely.

"We should make a fire to keep warm," Harry suggested sitting on the other side of Lisa, watching the boats in the marina bob up and down, the waves lapped peacefully and splashed the hull weakly.

Dylan strongly protested, "What about the policemen? They'll be back in a heartbeat if they saw a fire."

"Well then, let's move out. I know how to manoeuvre the boat, my parents have shown me. It's easy."

Lisa jumped up with delight, "Aww Harry. You're such a talented boyfriend!"

Dylan feeling rather hurt crossly stood up, then in an attempt to also impress Lisa he suggested, "I don't know about a fire. But what about candles? There's some below deck."

Lisa squealed with excitement, "Great idea Dylan, let's go get a box. Harry, you can get the boat going."

Harry didn't want Dylan going down into the boat with his girlfriend, angrily he pulled hard at the ropes and undid the knots. With the Maid of Splendour safely unmoored, he pushed the gear into the forward position and chugged her gracefully out towards sea. After about fifteen minutes he stopped the boat and lowered the anchor, just as the others returned.

"You were a long time!" He irritably snapped, snatching the box from Lisa.

Lisa brushed him aside and pushed the sticks into the wooden holders, "Sorry darling. We couldn't find the matches anywhere."

Dylan followed her around the deck like a puppy, lighting each candle individually with his lighter.

Lisa however continued to shiver, and she suddenly exclaimed, "I think we're going to need more candles. It's freezing up here."

Harry snorted loudly as she snatched the empty box back, "We don't need more candles, Lisa! There should be spare blankets in the bedroom at the back."

"Yes, we do need more candles!" she argued back, completely ignoring his suggestion about the blankets, as she swung the cabin-door open and climbed down, "There should be another box in the spare cupboard."

Dylan laughed as he lit the last candle on deck, "Feisty. I miss that about Lisa."

"Yeah? Well tough. She's my girlfriend now not yours, you'll do well to remember that!" Harry retorted, pushing the blankets on deck into a heap.

"Only because you charmed her with your good looks…brains…not so much."

"What and you're the intelligent one, are you? I'm the one that's always there for her and takes her out. What have you done recently...oh yeah! Nothing!"

"Because I have a job unlike you! At least I can pay to take Lisa out to nice places!"

Harry kicked out his legs as he shakily stood up, "Yeah...well. You know what...forget it."

The two men sat next to each other staring out to sea as the boat rocked up and down on the swell, both too drunk and exhausted to argue over such a trivial matter. St Heliers looked completely different at night, the city lights shone like stars and the funfair brightly illuminated the pier.

Dylan suddenly whiffed the air and spun his head from side to side, "Do you smell smoke?"

"Sorry, that's me," Harry answered, holding up his fag, "Want one?"

"Something's burning. JAYSUS HARRY! THE BOAT! THE BOAT IS ON FIRE!"

"WHAT!?" Harry exclaimed, hurriedly jumping up and straightaway fell backwards, hitting his head on the rail and groaned in pain. "BUCKETS! GRAB THOSE BUCKETS DYLAN! FILL THEM UP AND START THROWING!"

Without wasting a second Dylan unwound the rope holding the bucket in place and threw it over the side, the alcohol had now started to seep into his brain cells, *"DAMN! HARRY! I LOST IT! I LOST THE RUDDY BUCKET!"*

"FORGET IT DYLAN! GET ANOTHER BUCKET AND DON'T LET GO OF THE ROPE THIS TIME!" *Harry bellowed back, throwing some water over the fire but to no avail. The flames were hungrily eating up the paper streamers and dashed across the boat at an alarming speed. One of the blankets caught alight with an almighty whoosh, as the fire soon reached its fullest height. The rope attached to the anchor caught fire. Dylan launched forward with a bucket to put it out and immediately stumbled, as yet another wave crashed into the Maid of Splendour. Reaching out over the top of the rail he managed to grab a hold of the anchor rope just in the nick of time, but the fire was too strong and instantly burnt his hand. Dylan's reflexes kicked in and he released his grip. With only the rail to now hold onto and finding himself almost hanging upside down, he felt himself tipping off the boat and falling down into the icy waters below. Harry was quick to notice his friend bobbing deliriously in the water,*

"DYLAN! HANG ON!"

Dylan opened an eye as the sea smacked him about, something red and rubbery landed next to him, instinct told him to climb onto it. Harry relieved to see his friend safe in the dinghy revolved himself back to the battle and faced the flames head on. Half the boat was engulfed, there was no hope of saving her now.

"DYLAN!" Harry shouted over the side, in a hope that his friend could hear him, "KEEP THE DINGHY CLOSE BY, THERE'S A PADDLE ON THE SIDE. I'M GOING TO GET LISA, JUST WAIT THERE!"

Dylan didn't hear him, the night had been too much of an ordeal and the soothing waves had rocked him soothingly to sleep. Back on the boat, Harry clambered with speed over the cindering rails towards the cabin-door on the top deck, he flung it back open with force and climbed down.

"LISA! WAKE UP! THE BOAT IS ON FIRE!" Harry shouted, trying to shake her awake from where she slept peacefully on the bed. A massive bang sounded from outside and shook the boat and worsened Harry's fears. Immediately he felt a sick feeling in the pit of his stomach. Hurriedly he ran back to the ladder and looked up, the cabin-door had slammed itself shut. Harry banged with force and rammed his shoulder onto the closed door, but the door stubbornly refused to budge, and he only managed to bruise himself considerably. The darkness grew darker, the air grew smokier, to sleep was such a good thing right now. He curled up next to where Lisa lay and closed his eyes.

*

"What about Dylan sir? Do you still think he's behind The Marina Murders?" Constable Wright keenly asked, picking up on my hard stare in Dylan's direction.

I simply frowned and sighed with defeat, "I know he did it Wright. I simply know it."

About the Author

J.M.G.Smith grew up in the Chilterns and is where she got her inspiration and ideas for many of her characters. The ideas for picturesque scenery and panorama sea views came from her many travels to seaside villages surrounded by cliffs. Originally a keen gardener, she learnt horticulture at the Berkshire College of Agriculture before taking up the trade landscaping. J.M.G.Smith now lives in Nottingham with her husband and four children and has settled down to domestic duties, pot gardening at home and busily writing her next book.

Printed in Great Britain
by Amazon